THE ILLUSTRATED ULYSSES S. GRANT IN CHINA & Other Stories

BY TOM DURWOOD

Beautifully written ... a fantastic voyage around the world.
-- Claire Middleton, Goodreads

Tom Durwood just may have made a short-story fan out of me!
-- Tabitha Parkes, Goodreads, Indie Book Reviewer

ISBN Illustrated USG in China print
978-1-952520-10-5

ISBN Illustrated USG in China ebook
978-1-952520-11-2

Published by the Empire Studies Press

www.empirestudiespress.com
www.usginchina.com

This book is dedicated to BLF.

THE ILLUSTRATED ULYSSES S. GRANT IN CHINA

AND OTHER STORIES

by Tom Durwood

ILLUSTRATED BY
Zelda Devon
Sigurd Fenstrom
Timothee Mathon
Dominik Mayer
Boell Oyino
Kurt Uchman
Well-bee

ULYSSES S. GRANT IN CHINA
1879

FAMILIES FROM ALL OVER THE WORLD HAD COME TO CALIFORNIA.
GRASS FOR CATTLE AND WHEAT FOR BREAD, THE SOILS NURTURED WHATEVER MAN PLANTED.
WHEAT AND CORN WERE GROWING ON A SCALE UNKNOWN SINCE THE INLAND EMPIRES OF THE ANCIENT MAYA. NOW MEN CLASHED OVER THE HARVEST.

Front cover illustration by Well-bee.
Illustrations pages 11, 41, 43, 49 copyright © 2017 Edmund Liang.
Illustrations pages 13-18 copyright © 2021 Dominik Meyer.
Illustrations pages 24-28 copyright © 2021 Sigurd Fernstrom,
Illustrations pages iv and 81-98 copyright © 2021 Boell Oyino.
Illustration page 38 by Kirk Shinmoto.
Illustrations pages 51-74 copyright © 2017 Well-Bee.
Illustrations pages 114, 117, 122, 131, 140 copyright © 2021 Zelda Devon.
Illustrations pages v, 105, 116, 120, 124 copyright © 2021 Timothee Mathon.
Illustrations pages 112, 117, 139 copyright © 2021 Kurt Uchman.
Illustration page 22 copyright © 2017 Oscar Gregeborn.
"Succession" art page 35 by Pedro Kruger.
Portraits pages 29, 44 by Ryan Pallett.
Ships at sea illustration page 104, 147 by Yu Yu Ming
Illustration page 109 by Angela Sung
Front cover illustration by Well-bee

Photography credits

Page 21 ... Paintings in the Lascaux caves of France. Source: Wikimedia Commons
Page 32 ... Maya tablets. Source: Wikimedia Commons
Page 46 ... Benin sculptures Source: Wikimedia Commons
Page 77 ... Binenhof 1651 by Van Bassen. Source: Wikimedia Commons
Page 87 ... California Seal, State of California Capitol Museum
Source: Wikimedia Commons
Page 101 ... Frederic Remington's "Shotgun Hospitality (1908)
Source: Wikimedia Commons
Page 135 ... Map of Japan and Ryuku Islands, 18th century. Source: Wikimedia Commons
Page 143 ... USG photo with Li Hong Zhang. U.S. Embassy and Consulate in China.
Page 145 ... Japan warship illustration, Massachusetts Institute of Technology.
Source: Wikimedia Commons
Page 139 ... Qing dynasty banner Source: Wikimedia Commons

Book design by Dennis Umaly and Kelley Creative

CONTENTS

A NOTE FROM THE AUTHOR

You are reading an Advance Reader Copy (ARC) of this book, which is scheduled for publication on June 8, 2021. Thank you for your interest in my work! ARCs are often not fully refined and may contain minor errors.

As an advance reader, I invite you to share your feedback and commentary with me at tdurwood@gmail.com. Also, in exchange for receiving this free advance copy, I encourage you to leave a review of the book on Goodreads at goodreads.com/book/show/57321438-the-illustrated-ulysses-s-grant-in-china-and-other-stories. Honest reviews are the number one tool for independent authors like me to reach our audience with literary work they'll appreciate.

Thanks for reading. Enjoy the stories!

Stay tuned for my trilogy, *The Illustrated Colonials,* which is on schedule for a July 4th release.

You may also like *The Illustrated Boatman's Daughter*, available from all major booksellers.

Best,

Tom Durwood
www.boatmansdaughter.com
www.empirestudiespress.com
www.kidlitcrit.com

[This page intentionally left blank.]

The Origins of Civilization

Around the year 10,000 B.C., somewhere in the
Tigris-Euphrates basin, the first farmer planted seeds,
and grew a crop. The world of hunter-gatherers
– and of all civilization – would change forever.

-- *The Rand McNally Atlas of World History*

Art by Dominik Mayer
Coloring by Javelin Studio

"YOU LOOK LIKE ONE OF THOSE big hogs we killed," said the bully Cor to the girl Ydra.

"You worry that, because you are so ugly, none of the men will mate with you. I will take pity on you," he said, as if it were a friendly thing.

"Well now," replied the girl coolly, looking up as she prepared the food for the clan's dinner. "That is certainly something to look forward to." But what she meant was, *Try it and I'll kill you.*

Cor just laughed. "It won't be long now."

He chomped on one of the fruits and moved on.

"Ignore him," said her mother, Yn. "He's an idiot."

But he is a very strong idiot, the girl did not say.

"Press harder when you stir," advised Yn.

"I am!" said the girl, Ydra, irritated.

"There must not be any lumps. The first people," by which term she meant the members of the clan, "hate that."

"Yes."

"They hate lumps. They think they are bugs."

"Mother!"

"If there are lumps they won't eat it."

"Leave me alone!"

"All right. Did you see the red globes? They are so soft. I wonder why. Are they ripe? I better go out to get some more of the purple shade, we'll need more for the stew. Remember to stir the pot. Every so often."

"I know, Mother."

"So none of it blackens." She took the carved wooden spoon and demonstrated.

"Yes, I *know*, Mother -- "

Yn ignored her. "I'll be back soon."

* * *

"What can I do?" Yn asked the radish.

The tribeswoman held the reddish bulb before her, inspecting its size and roundness and color and the texture of its skin. She tried to see inside it, so she could understand it.

"How can I make you grow better?"

She looked up at the tree branches partially shading her garden.

Too much sun? Not enough sun?

She picked up an unfamiliar plant. She took a bite of it and instantly spit it out. *Terrible!* How can it look so pretty and taste so bad? What kind of totem is that?

There must be a way to tell …

She saw tracks of small beasts in the earth. They came at night, attracted by the apparently prized plants she had in her collection.

"Everyone wants your magic, *ayala*," she said to the radish.

To protect her growing garden, she would reinforce the crude fence. She could raise its height and reinforce the joints, which she knew were feeble.

Ydra would help.

Ydra would understand at once.

Ydra was clever, more so than Yn herself.

Is it too late today?

Tomorrow, first thing tomorrow …

Yes, a stronger fence. Tomorrow. Perhaps Eosa will help.

Even better if she could devise some sort of trap. *A series of traps for the invading animals.* The clan could feed off of them as well …

The hunter Cor glimpsed Yn talking to her plants, down among the garden rows.

The hunter saw her moving in the sunlight reflected off the waters. The woman was tending her ridiculous plants, in the gardens, just up from the banks of the river, beneath the distant blue-white walls of ice.

No one else was near.

Just the two of them.

Being in no way a reflective man, Cor decided he may just as well murder Yn.

He preferred to kill Eosa, but Eosa was too popular.

Cor was tired of this skinny Yn and her high-minded ways. Yn and her homely daughter. Yn pretended to obey the will of the clan, but she was independent. She acted as if she were an ordinary woman of the clan, but Cor saw her defiance shining in her eyes and in her every gesture. Cor abused her at every opportunity, and punished the daughter even worse. He wanted to kill them both.

Cor decided he may just as well murder Yn.

She should die today, realized Cor. *Right now. She and her ugly girl.*

Eosa, the clan's leader, protected Yn.

Eosa protected Yn because she had saved the life of his son during the hunt of the elk herd, using a *datura* poultice to cleanse the boy's wounds and a balm of powdered yarrow roots to banish his fever. Her acrid plant magic had brought the boy back from death.

Worse – far, far worse -- the woman Yn had told Eosa that they could eat some of these same plants: that they could live on meal made from the flowers and weeds which she cultivated.

She had been having dreams – visions, really – since the tribe's diet had changed. In her visions, she saw a multitude of people like herself, assembled, for some purpose. She saw smooth-skinned trees towering over the steppes, and smooth walls, and long grasses down the slope to the living waters of the river. She felt sure that it all meant something, something important, that it held some vital message for her, even though she could not say what.

More and more, she felt that this garden contained her destiny.

She mixed the plant cereal with meat; then, as the tribe accepted the strange taste, she served the pulverized grains with spices, and in stew, and baked flat.

No one had taken particular note. Though unpleasant, the coarse gruel filled the stomach.

Late one night, Yn had taken Eosa and his mate to the riverbank and showed them where she had dropped seeds the previous autumn, when they had passed this way on their migration to the steppes, following the herds. Now, two seasons later, green shoots of comfrey and durmast sprouted up from the soil. She explained that the totem of this specific land apparently made it possible to create the plants you wanted.

Eosa did not understand.

"I can grow food for our people," Yn had told him. "The seeds sleep in the ground over the winter, then grow again. For us to eat."

It had been a terrible autumn, and an even worse winter. Hunting had gone well at first, but then the elk did not want to die. An ill-conceived chase of a giant herd of mammoths had been a disaster. The winter had been colder than any they could remember. They had lost a quarter of the clan in the high-mountain snow drifts, and four hunters to a week-long pursuit of the wounded calf.

One more season like that and there would be no clan members left.

The hunters said they knew more now, they had a better idea of where the game would travel and how to trap and kill them, but no one really believed it.

They returned to the cave by the two streams. It was one of those pockets of boreal forest where a lush green valley formed by the glacial runoff gave them rich soils as well as a steady supply of lesser-game visitors, animals which stopped for the water.

It was not a difficult decision to stay.

At first, the soils had been too moist. The plants died. Yn directed them to carry the plants in clay containers and arranged them in garden rows, tucked in the flats among the rocks.

Legumes seemed to attract the wild goats, and the clan liked goat meat.

Yn and Ydra experimented with different combinations of herbs, and which berries to forage, and how best to summon each plant's spirit.

How the seeds had grown!

So, on the eve of the new moon, with the clan growing fat on Yn's berries and plants, and with six women carrying children, Eosa announced that there would be no wandering this autumn.

The clan would remain in the Gray Caves through this season and the winter, rather than chase game over the steppes. When Cor asked what they would do for food, the answer came quickly:

Yn's gardens.

In summer, the meadows of grass would attract grazing game. In the winter, water-formed gorges and caves would protect them from the cold. They would burn wood from the trees of the loess forest. And they would eat Yn's plants.

Eating grass! Like rabbits!

Cor was pleased to put an end to it.

Now, as he crawled through the long grass, he smiled to himself, pleased at the thought of clan life returned to normal, hunting and wandering across the lands of Ymir. Cor liked meat. He understood where it came from. The gods liked it when they killed game. The spirit of the animal he ate gave him strength.

Eating plants was unacceptable.

I will end this now, he told himself as he tracked silently through the long grass toward the stream.

The woman Yn was trimming herbs with her hand-axe, bunching them to dry.

That the plants themselves carried her power had not dawned on Cor. That the herbs and grains would live on, heedless of human treachery, needing only an acolyte to extract their power.

Not that he cared. His act of murder would return him to clan leader, and return the clan to its natural life.

He looked around once more, to make sure they were alone. Her cries would be drowned out by the river. He advanced, unworried when she noticed him in the dancing sunlight …

* * *

In the great cave, the girl Ydra saw Cor return.

She noted the scratch on the bully's arm, and the bold way he entered.

Ydra made sure to concentrate on mashing the grains into meal for dinner.

The fire burned low.

They would serve the pulverized grains with spices, in a stew.

Her mother, Yn, had left at dawn to tend the gardens, down by the stream. The hunter Cor had left soon after. Now it was evening and Cor was back, mingling with the others. He nursed a bloody gash along one forearm. Her mother was nowhere to be seen.

Cor looked directly across the cave at Ydra. It was not an accidental or casual glance but a purposeful glare, as though marking her, measuring her position.

Ydra kept her head down as she worked. Her mother often wandered far from the caves, searching for new plants. No reason to sound an alarm for her, not yet.

Everyone knew that Cor despised the plants.

The garden meant they could stop wandering and stay in one place. Build shelters. Teach the young ones, instead of dragging them across the steppes. Now some of the women had taken to drawing on the walls with color from the plants.

A lark's whistle floated into the cave and echoed, sweet and clear, off the walls.

The girl's skin went cold.

It was her mother's signal.

The call sounded again: *She sounds so weak … but she is alive.*

Ydra reached over to her pouch and added a yellow weed, *spikenard,* to the grain meal, just a little, at the edge of the shallow bowl. No one else had noticed. The girl chopped it patiently: the plant would release more of its potency if she ground it fine. She heard Cor laughing with Eosa at some crude jest.

Yn had warned her daughter of the danger which the seeds carried, for they held powerful spirits within them -- crops to eat, herbs to heal. And wherever power lived, jealousy and bloody death would always follow.

Her mother had taught her to hide her thoughts.

Ydra eyed Cor across the fire. The girl understood what had happened. She would bide her time, just a little longer. Her mother had shown her, once, as calmly as feeding a baby, what spikenard will do to a man.

Ydra had waited. A good hunter is patient.

She had seen visions in her dreams, too.

A potent poison, the powdered spikenard, when mixed with liquid, would tighten the bully's throat until the sun burst inside the victim's skull.

It would happen quickly.

Now Ydra hummed as she worked.

No one could stop it. Even if they knew what was happening

Ydra tossed in green shoots to mask its taste. She added a fistful of berries.

Tonight the bully would pay. For all those insults. All that abuse.

Tonight Cor, who had failed to conceive the problem, would die. She would watch from a distance – not too close, but close enough to see his anguish in detail. Perhaps he would notice her and realize.

Tonight Cor, who had failed to conceive the problem, would die.

The fire flared.

Once he was gone, they would double the size of the gardens.

Ydra crushed the berries which would mask the poison's taste.

She watched closely. The crimson-purple juice slid down the side of the bowl.

Oh, Cor will enjoy his dinner …

AFTERWORD

Appr. 10,000 B.C.
Mesopotamia
The first farmer plants seeds, fights off evil, and begins civilization.

Many years ago, I ran across this suggestive passage in a Rand McNally history of the world:

> "Around the year 10,000 B.C., somewhere in the Tigris-Euphrates basin, the first farmer planted seeds, and grew a crop. The world of hunter-gatherers – and of all civilization – would change forever."

This story is my version of how that might have gone.

It's possible I will extend this story fragment, since I like these two cranky women. I would need to figure out a plotline that has some originality; the second Maya story seems awfully similar to what this would be.

* * *

Anthropologists believe that early man tended to gather in nomadic groups and chase game around. That fast, harsh strategy of existence made them more comparable to a herd of wolves than to us; the constant demands of moving and hunting left no time to develop written language, alphabets, ideas, devices, inventions (you can't think when you are running all day). Only cities gave us the time to do all those things, and cities did not really exist because you could not keep all those stationery people fed. You could not stop chasing across the plains.

Until the first farmer.

It was the act (or should I say the concept) of cultivating crops which led to villages and animals in pens. Things of that nature. Only then did men and women have the time to record images in paintings on cave walls, and devise symbols, and organize their thoughts into religions, or architecture, or any of the other traditions of civilization.

Once farmers of the Levant tended gardens of barley, lentils and chickpeas, a stable food supply enabled populations to explode, and small cave=bound groups turned into sprawling kingdoms. "It's a part of the story of civilization that we're just beginning to understand," writes Iosif Lazaridis, a postdoctoral researcher at Harvard Medical School.

Paintings in the Lascaux caves of France. Wikimedia Commons

CHARACTERS
Ydra is a smart, resilient girl whom the clan hunters jeer as ugly. Her mother is a very tough lady named Yn. Together, Yn and Ydra dream about a new life for her clan, one where the plants which they harvest give rise to a new existence.

In earlier drafts, Ydra was more active; now the action all comes to her. Ydra patiently sits at her mortar and pestle, gathering understanding before she takes a decisive step in the clan's destiny.

The Jade Necklace

One of the great mysteries in the
New World history; the apparently spontaneous
collapse of Classic Maya civilization during the
ninth and tenth centuries ...

-- Ronald Wright,
Time Among the Maya

Art by Sigurd Fenstrom

Hidden in the flickering

shadows, the young adventurer heard the sounds of struggle echo off the stone walls of the belly of the Palace of Seven Moons.

He crept forward carefully, stepping so softly that he could listen, but he could not be heard. He had not survived so many deadly encounters in his young life by giving away his position.

He heard a knife clatter to the ground, followed by an obscene laugh.

He turned a corner in those dank dungeons and saw it --

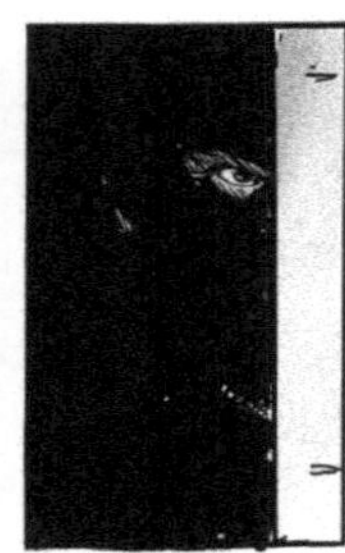

It was a gaggle of the imperial guards. He saw an arched juncture or hallway where several passages met, and dimly-lit stairs beyond; the very place he had been trying to find.

He counted five men. They were close. He heard their laughter clearly now.

He could not make out what they were doing until his eyes adjusted to the bright pool of light beneath the mounted torches which illuminated them. The five men had pinned a wriggling prisoner against the stone walls; now they laughed at the prisoner's vain struggles. They took turns slapping the helpless figure.

A girl --

Now the young mercenary could hear her wicked curses. He did not like what he saw, yet he was almost relieved: he had been stealing, mapless, through the dark mazelike dungeons beneath the palace for almost an hour. The unnatural silence had begun to trouble him; his people were more used to windy mountains and wild lands than to these dank man-made passageways which crept and wandered with no apparent design.

"Let me go!" she now commanded. "Don't touch me— "

The guards were drunk. He studied their thick, slow motions.

The girl let her legs go and sank to the floor and almost crawled out of her captors' grasp – but they were too many for her.

They were too drunk to stop themselves.

The girl would soon meet her ancestors.

The thief took an extra moment to watch each man, to see how he moved, to capture his rhythm.

With a low laugh, he stepped into the center of the passageway.

"Come, brothers," he bellowed. He banged his blade against the stone wall. "Here is better sport."

"Come, brothers." He banged his blade against the stone wall. "Here is better sport ..."

* * *

These were lawless times. The kingdoms of Ek were disintegrating. The Maya had greatly displeased the gods, who had punished them since the Spring, when the corn had first gone bad.

The adventurer had left his own tribes to serve in the emperor's pay. He had been satisfied with good wages; then he lost his taste for slaughtering farmers and peasants.

In a tavern earlier that night, the adventurer had overheard a drunken Scythian describe the treasure in Lord Ek's trove, in particular a necklace of jade ovals. The Scythian had detailed the necklace's ancient origins and its present location, until he was distracted by a green-eyed serving girl. The young mercenary had decided on the spot to steal it; and now he stood directly below the chambers where the necklace lay.

* * *

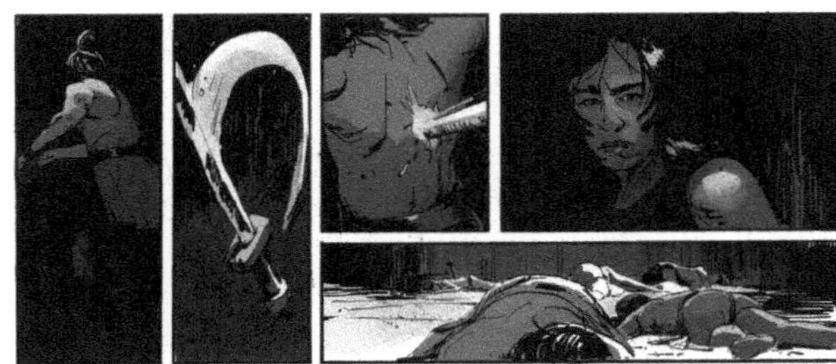

Tired of watching, the adventurer rushed the soldiers.

He was upon them in four steps.

The sword in his hand flashed: he gutted the largest member of the guard.

Before that body struck the stone floor, his gleaming blade severed the second man's head: the third he grabbed by the neck and, lifting a corded arm, snapped the man's neck.

The fourth and fifth guardsmen held back. He motioned for them to advance.

They fled.

Snatching a blade from the dead man, he flung it and saw the fourth man fall gurgling to the stone floor.

The girl struggled, coughing, to her feet.

For a long moment, the adventurer studied her face and the heaving surface of her torn tunic.

By the markings along her neckline and by the strong forearms and tanned face, he saw that she was from one of the farmer clans. Captured and offered for the amusement of Ek and his lechers, perhaps.

Her features seemed familiar.

* * *

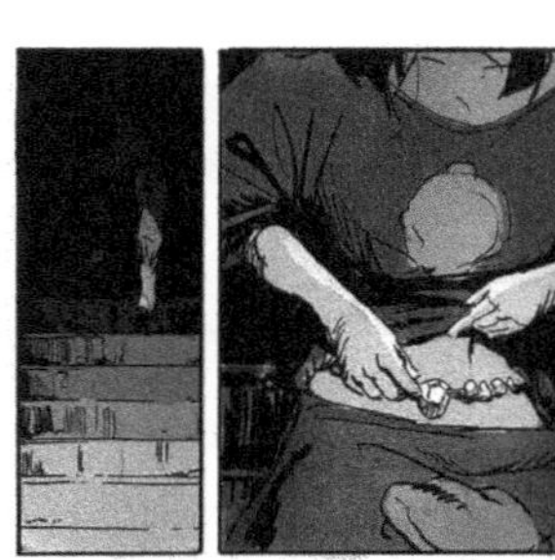

The Tiller girl looked closely at the adventurer.

His chest rose and fell as he inspected her in the sharply shadowed light.

A copper band graced the upper part one arm. A freeman. One of the mountain tribes, probably.

The prophecies had not mentioned him …

It had begun with a blight.

The edges of the maize had started turning brown two months earlier.

The corn's husk, its clean silky green sheathing, was compromised.

Tainted.

They reviewed all their irrigation methods for an answer, the soil, the moon and stars. No new insects. It was an act of the gods. Some new cycle had begun, two cycles above the *alautun*. Some silent click in the sky.

The ruination of the High Maya civilization had begun.

"It's the Fifth Lord," the shaman had told them that night. "He rises from his slumbers. He wants the city. Our time has come."

The Tillers would find a new home, new soils for their rows of vegetables and grains, perhaps in the hills north of Four Turtle, and east.

This girl's father, Chieftain of the Tillers, ordered that the entire crop be burned in a great bonfire.

A toddler managed to find a discarded husk and used it for teething. She was in seizures by nightfall, dead still by sunrise.

The Tiller Chieftain went to warn the Emperor. But Lord Ek and all his advisors could not see the blight, and thus did not believe in its existence. They politely dismissed the Chieftain, keeping the clan's *Kinich Ahau*, or talisman.

The Jade Necklace.

The ruination of the High Maya civilization had begun.

The necklace was an heirloom. The gemstone was said to have been forged in the fires of G Three, the Jaguar God of Fire (also patron of the number Seven). The jade carried inside it the protection of their ancestors. The clanswomen told stories around the fires of its history, tracing its lineage through the wars of the Hero Twins and the eventful life of an obscure daughter of the Rain Deity named Ix Chel.

Soon the Kingdoms of Copal would be engulfed by lunacy and death such as Gilgamesh never saw. Soon, bodies would pile up in the obsidian quarries, and scatter on the steps of the stone pyramids.

But they needed the *Kinich Ahau*.

The Jade Necklace was a talisman. It brought them more than luck, it brought them the favor of the gods. The tribe must carry it with them to their new home to have any chance of survival.

Lord Ek kept the Jade Necklace in his palace, hostage to his greed.

The girl made it her mission to retrieve the necklace for her people.

She had served tables in three taverns before she overheard its mention.

* * *

"Come with me," said the Adventurer to the girl he had just saved. "We'll raid the palace trove."

A warm smile took shape in her features, starting in her eyes and spreading to her sun-kissed cheeks, until it reached her parted lips, suggesting more riches than a man could find in any king's trove.

"Come with me, boy," she said, leaning her body close against him. "We'll enjoy the night."

Such a warrior could help her family make the trek to the new home, through bandit-filled lowlands and the Three-Jaguar regions, where thieves and cut-throats lurked along all roads and most pathways.

The boy paused, as though trying to place her.

Then the white of his teeth appeared beneath the shaggy black mane. He kissed her and laughed, a vibrant sound that echoed loud in those lifeless halls, a sound rich with youth and the promise of life lived to the brim.

He disappeared into the darkness – for a moment – and then emerged into half-light to vault the stairs, three at a time.

Her green eyes watched him go.

The sub-palace corridors were once again silent. Light from the torch flames flickered, casting their shifting patterns. She could see him no more, nor hear his footfalls.

The girl paused.

He will only find a hornet's nest …

One of the guards on the floor moaned. She swept her knife from the floor and delivered a short, savage blow; he moaned no more.

She returned the knife to the slim pouch at her waist.

She touched the smooth jade of the necklace draped low around her waist.

She turned and ran easily towards a shorter hallway, one that led to a portal and a garden, and then beyond that to grassy paths and open plazas and farmlands, squatting safe and green beneath the snowy mountains beyond.

AFTERWORD

Approximately 890 A.D.
The Yucatan Peninsula
The High Maya Empire begins to crumble; its leaders go mad from the wheat blight.
A teen adventurer invades the royal palace of the crumbling Maya Kingdom, in search of treasure. He finds something else.

Long ago, I ran across a *National Geographic* article suggesting that the High Maya civilization crumbled because of the lack of genetic diversity among the maize (corn) plants. Since all the maize was genetically identical, once a single plant became infected, the pathogen would zip across the entire nation. A mighty empire lost to botany. And we are all familiar with the terrible story of how, six hundred years later, the Spanish priest Diego de Landa destroyed over 90 per cent of the Mayan writings, essentially disappearing that culture's collected wisdom and mathematics. Double-lost.

Both characters get names in the longer adventure.

CHARACTERS
The Adventurer has a back-story in the longer version. It has been jettisoned in this shorter version, in favor of the story's velocity.

The girl gets much more room to fill out as a character in the longer story. As you can guess, she is part of a farming clan that becomes the "point of the spear" when crops fail. She is stealing the jade necklace to finance her family's relocation to higher ground. No one knows what it all means … except her.

* * *

This is the second in a cycle of botany-based stories. I have come to like this as a stand-alone tale. It is a fragment of a longer narrative about how a group of young Mayans might have escaped the empire's collapse, carrying with them:

a) a small cache of healthy seeds, and
b) all of the magical Mayan mathematics tables, thus
saving them for a later, wiser time. *Heh heh.*

Recently, drought has also been mentioned as a factor in the Maya collapse, but I was unable to make that work in my little version.

I am currently exploring an epic expansion and extension of this short story. These same two characters escape the failing kingdom and head for the hills encountering perils (both human and otherwise). They serve as a backstory for a modern-day detective case. The theme is the same: an empire's first job is to feed its people. When that breaks down, society falls. The parallels to the Irish Potato Famine (which suffered from the same fatal single-genetic-species model), the little-known Chinese famine of 1958-1962, and the current crisis of disappearing biodiversity are compelling.

If you like this style of writing, I recommend Robert E. Howard's *Moon of Skulls, The Complete Conan of Cimmeria,* and *The Savage Tales of Solomon Kane*, which features some wicked illustrations by Gary Gianni. A book called *Time of the Maya* by a good, good writer named Ronald Wright is a window into Mayan culture, then and now.

* * *

Today, our cities are in crisis. More than half the world's population now lives in cities, yet the quality of life in our poorly-designed urban centers can be polluted, dangerous and precarious. We live in overly dense centers, sharply segregated into neighborhoods of terrible disparity.

Mesoamerican cities were much smarter. The cities of the diverse tribes of what we now call Central America -- including the Maya, Aztec, Olmec, Toltec and others -- featured more "green space" than buildings, and lots of urban agriculture.

Maya tablets featured art, astrology, and numbers.Source: Wikimedia Commons

In Teotihuacan, wealth differences were quite small. The people of the Aztec City Calixtlahuaca (population over 200,000) lived in three-hundred-unit apartment compounds and traveled on raised causeways 60 meters wide and four miles long. Systems of moats and earthworks bordered the cities, to protect against invaders. Surrounding farmland needed to support an urban population was strictly managed, so everyone ate well.

We have a great deal to learn from these past cultures.

For further reading, check out my open-access journal feature on Michael E. Smith, "An Introduction to Mesoamerica" (www.empirestudies.com).

GRUPO OESTE
GRUPO CENTRAL
A MERIDA
CAMPAMENTO
A CAMPECHE
SACBE-1

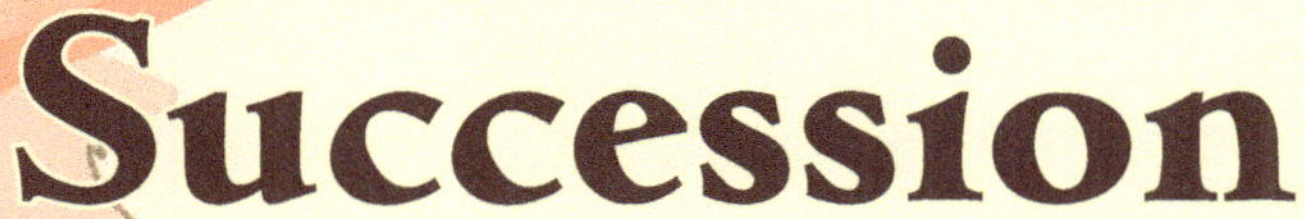

Succession

... By the time a warrior had undergone the preparatory rituals for combat, he was set apart from peaceful society, bound to his fellows by the tightest emotional bonds, and the powerful taboos that surrounded him could only be expiated in the terrible excitement of combat.

— Ludwig Alberti,
Account of the Tribal Life and Customs of the Xhosa in 1807

Art by Pedro Kruger

Flickering firelight

illuminated the boy's face from one side, the even light of the rising sun illuminated the other. Strokes of a brightly colored brush flickered over his black skin. The surface of his cheekbones was so black that the white and then red and then blue lines of paint popped out in vivid contrast. The skin twitched.

"Stand still," admonished the mother.

"Do I look fearsome?" asked the youth.

The pair were a still portrait amidst the commotion around them.

"Aye," replied the mother. "You are a mighty Oyo warrior. All the world will know, by your markings, and by your brave deeds."

The boy grunted with satisfaction.

As she finished painting, his entire was altogether magnificent in its patterns and tribal symbols, markings which announced his rank and identity.

The youth was handsome and impossibly young.

"Kamau, you must listen to every word that Kunle teaches you—"

"Kunle! Bah! He is fat! And boring! I should be going with my father –"

"The first thing a warrior learns is obedience!" she reprimanded. "Are you the spoiled chieftain's son? You want special treatment? Is that how you will rule when it comes your turn?"

"No," her son answered sullenly.

This doting mother and her eager young warrior were part of a crowded village preparing for a great hunt, families fussing over the young hunters about to take their first patrol. The village had assembled to see them off.

"Watch out for the big cats," she said. "One of D'Sheza's buffaloes had a deep scar. The cats are out for blood. Boars, too. Boars are worse."

"I am a killer! They better watch out for me! Short life! Sharp knife!"

"I see," The mother laughed gently. "It is not always so pleasant, growing up, Kamau," she murmured.

The face was done. It was harder to see how young he was.

"I love you, my little warrior."

"Mother! Stop -- "

"I hate it that you are so old."

The boy stood apart from her. He brandished his spear, and shook it above his head.

* * *

Wind stirred the morning mists across the mysterious green mountainous landscape.

Rock formations towered in the middle distance. Beneath the foothills where the rhythmic sound of running emerged, visible from the footpaths, lay a valley partially obscured by fog. The runners caught glimpses of antelope grazing at grass along a riverbed their curved horns dipping as they grazed. One of them looked up at the passing patrol.

"Look how light the grasses are. Drought changes everything. Even the beasts are not themselves."

Kunle, the Oyo leader, a short, boring man with a round belly, lectured as they loped in the morning, tossing comments over his shoulder. His three charges – Kamau, the chieftain's son, and his boyhood friends, talkative Gyasi and tall Danjuma -- were slim apprentice warriors who paid attention only intermittently as they moved easily over the terrain.

"It is not always so pleasant, growing up," she murmured.

"If we are attacked at the front of the column," called the leader.

"Three and four, retreat and circle," retorted the boys.

"'Shields up'!" corrected Kunle. "Then 'retreat and circle.' If we are attacked at the rear of the column …"

"Shields up," they answered. "One and two, retreat and circle."

"If we are attacked in the middle of the column …" called Kunle.

"Shields up," replied the patrol. "One and four, retreat and circle.

As the patrol turned to cross the first rise they quickened the pace. Each of the four carried short spears easily in one hand: their faces were decorated with painted leopard spots and necklaces which accentuated the graceful motions of their loping run

Kunle slowed to inspect their running positions. It was their first patrol, and he wanted to make sure every detail was correct.

"Shields always up. Tuck your spear arm tight as you run, Kamau. You run protected. Like a turtle. Like this."

He demonstrated

"Sharp eyes," he urged the three boys.

"They will come out of the east and south. There."

The morning patrol turned upland and ran up the slope.

"The Edo are not in the habit of giving warnings before they attack."

A fierce enemy would soon cross that valley. Bloody wars of succession rocked the neighboring kingdoms. King Oranmiyan sought his nephew, a pretender to the throne, to make an agreement on the succession. But the nephew, Ila of Irangu, knew of this, and had deflected all communication. So Oranmiyan had sent the Edo, his legendary palace guard, to persuade the nephew, one way or another, to come to the table. All the villages of the Fulani and Songhai, shards of the Kanem-Bournou empire, watched with interest from the north and west to see who would emerge from Irangu.

The Edo had revolutionized warfare in the once-quiet kingdoms of the Niger valley. Their army was built on units called *amabutho,* or guilds, bands of warriors who had been summoned from the home villages at early ages. Their brigades were given a name, and a distinctive uniform, so that they came to refer to themselves by their *amabutho,* rather than their clan, names. Their military philosophy was simple: to eat up the enemy. Attack whenever possible.

"See the tracks," Kunle called. "The boars forage for water, and it is their mating season. They are surely crazed in these weeks."

"There!" hissed Gyasi, pointing to a gash in the walls of fog. "Is that a column of Edo?"

"Wildebeest, wonderful one," answered Kamau.

The three boys kept squinting into the distance, looking for signs of the enemy. Behind and below them, west of the riverbend, lay the Oyo village, a warren of huts surrounded by millet fields and patches of garden. Snowy mountains guarded the far distance, leagues beyond the village.

"Bend down when you cross the ridge! The whole valley can see you when you're skylined like that -- "

"I want them to see me," replied Gyasi. "I am a mighty slayer. The Edo will run for their huts."

"Yes," said Danjuma. "They have only to see you to be afraid."

"The Edo are not afraid of us," said Kamau. "We are farmers. We want to remain farmers. All they do is fight and kill. They are like a separate race. But we are not their enemy just now; they seek imperial rivals. Let us avoid them."

The boys glanced at one another: they considered this a weak statement of purpose.

"They say he has some of the Samburu among his ranks," commented Gyasi. "The ones with the neck rings."

"Huh. If I had an Edo here in front of me, and a sharp spear in my hand, then we would see a thing," bragged Kamau.

"Yes, we would," said Danjuma.

"Yes, we *would*," said Gyasi.

"I *know!*" said Danjuma.

"Hush," warned Kunle. "The Edo are always attacking. Always moving forward. If they encounter a tree that is in their way, they chop it down. If they come upon a river, they ford it. A tiger, they slay it."

His young charges contemplated this image.

"They stand together. They watch one another. A warrior will risk death rather than leave his brother in danger."

The trail appeared and disappeared beneath the steady pace of their running. The first morning turned easily into afternoon without event. On the second morning, they saw flocks of birds migrating eastward.

"Now Oranmiyan seeks his junior brother in Irangu," narrated Kunle as they loped along the rising trail.

"What for?" asked Kamau.

"Succession," answered Kunle. "It is a war of succession. A warrior keeps his shield up as he runs, Danjuma. There you are. Now, Oranmiyan is the last son of Odudwada. He needs to eliminate all pretenders to the throne."

"They do not seek war with us," continued Kunle. "Their fight is with Irangu, not us. But if we get in the fire's path, we will surely be burned. We want them to know we are here. That fighting us will cost them dearly. That way they will leave us alone."

Danjuma noticed how Kamau's hand looked gripping the spear as he ran: this looked strong to him, and manly, so he tried to hold his in the same way. Gyasi saw this and shoved Danjuma, knocking his shield cockeyed and disturbing his warriorly demeanor --

A sudden violent rush overtook them. A hideous roar devoured the quiet morning --

"Ugh --"

Danjuma went down. His shield would have saved him.

Squealing hideously, the wild boar gored the boy a second time, and savagely stomped him, and gored him a third time. The little pot-bellied man knocked the beast aside. Mad and wild, the mad boar attacked the Oyo warrior.

"Under your shields!" cried Kunle.

A sudden violent rush overtook them. A hideous roar devoured the quiet morning.

Kunle fell on the predator with his spear, which splintered on the beast's rough hide.

Without warning a second boar, even bigger and more rabid than the first, rushed Gyasi.

Gyasi, who was clever with his shield, blunted the attack but was thrown to the ground.

Kamau slammed his shield against the boar, trying to get the beast to stop goring Kunle.

Danjuma ducked into a shallow pitch and hid under his tipped-down shield.

Kamau, seeing that his blows had no effect, pivoted with all his might and drove a broken spearhead into the first beast's temple, where it lodged and then fell free. The blow merely slowed it: the predator gathered itself for a new charge.

The second beast rushed, pinning the little man against the tree trunk.

"—*Uuuunnnnnnngh*!" Kunle winced.

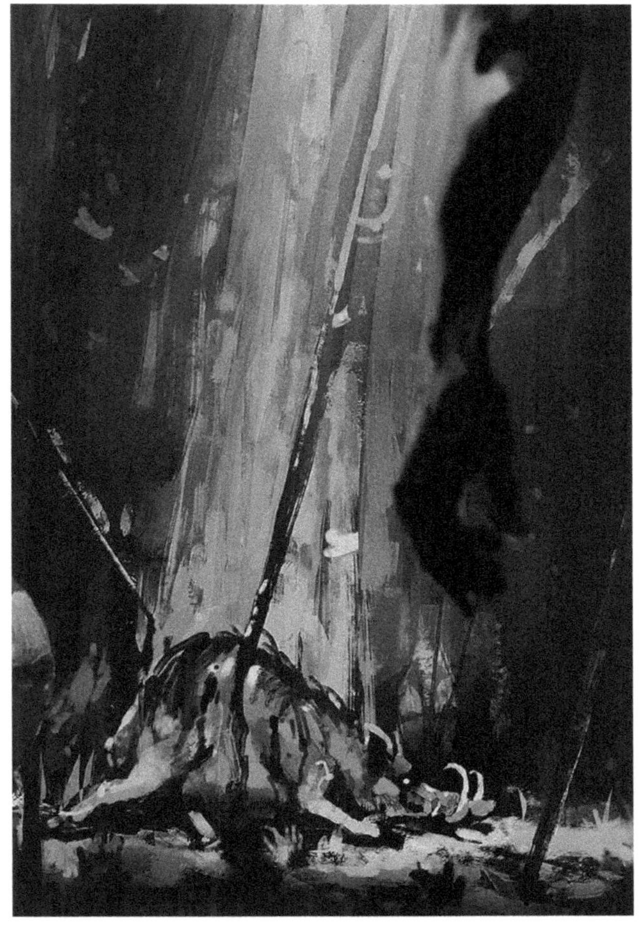

Gyasi, bloody and terrified, tried to rise and attack the boar but stumbled.

The beast gored Kunle in the stomach.

Suddenly a new figure flashed into the fray, swift and overwhelmingly powerful. It seized the second boar by the neck and somehow flung it away from Kunle, who was bloody and badly wounded. The prostate boar was punished with a volley of vicious blows until – incredibly -- its spine snapped.

An Edo warrior raised his head, huge and resplendent, a figure out of a dream, his skin black as burnt cork, his arms splattered with the beast's blood. A coil of feathers around his neck proclaimed him an attendant of the King. The exotic line of his facial paint and a carved bracelet at his wrist bespoke the artisanship of the splendid Benin civilization.

A third boar broke from the shrubs. The Edo swiveled and hurled his massive spear with impossible speed and force on a flat, cruel trajectory. The boar was skewered, shivering, against a tree trunk.

But he had overlooked the first boar. The snarling beast caught the warrior's leg and flipped him --

Danjuma rose from under his shield.

"AAAAAGH!! Die die die die –"

Terrified and sobbing, Danjuma smashed at the beast with the sharp edge of his shield: apprentice or no, he would take his part in this battle. The boar gave no quarter and lashed at the boy's arms. Danjuma suddenly saw pot-bellied Kunle, covered in blood, rise and knock the boar's legs aside.

Losing all control, the boy now hurled himself onto the huge animal like a berserker: Both hands on his shield, he slammed it on the bony head over and over. He managed through sheer manic energy to stun the predator.

The Edo stepped forward and, using Kunle's broken spear, poleaxed the beast with a single savage blow. He stamped on its shuddering neck.

All was still.

Danjuma suddenly saw pot-bellied Kunle, covered in blood, rise and knock the boar's legs aside.

The Edo stood upright. His right leg was bleeding from a bad gash.

He retrieved his spear from the tree trunk.

Kunle shivered and lay dead.

Danjuma was dead.

Gyasi was hurt but alive.

Kamau could not stop sobbing.

"What was his name?" asked the Edo.

"Ku – Ku – I can't – Kunle saved me--" gasped Kamau.

"Hush, little warrior. He was a brave leader."

"Is – is he – is he dead? I can't (gasp) -- "

"He died protecting his apprentices," said the Edo.

"I don't (gasp) -- my father (gasp) -- " Sobs racked the boy's chest, and tears ran down his cheeks. "I—I can't breathe – "

"You are Oyo. That is your village, yonder?"

"Aye."

"By your marking, you are the chieftain's son."

"Y-Yes – but I – "

The Edo broke a necklace off the dead man's neck and handed it to the boy. It was a leopard's face, rendered in bright small stones.

The boy's breathing began to ease.

He looked up into the enemy's eyes.

"When our column passes, tell your obas to stay west of the river. We won't come looking for you.

"Oranmiyan is in a hurry to engage the armies of Irango."

The Edo made a solemn gesture of brotherhood.

"Understand? It's you now. Your people need you."

Kamau took a deep breath and nodded. He did not understand anything.

He bent and helped Gyasi to his feet. He looked down at his dead leader's face. Kunle appeared calm, as though he knew he had met his responsibilities in this life.

When Kamau looked back up, a hint of composure, a hint of understanding of the terrible swiftness of life, had crept into his face.

The Edo was gone.

Kunle had given his life. That much Kamau knew.

Now he must bury Kunle deep in the ground, and Danjuma, and say a proper prayer over their graves, and mark them well, as young soldiers have done since the times of purple-shrouded Kemet, and Massinissa of Numidia, and Ijebu the Conqueror, and the warrior poet Antar, and stoic Abraha Al-Arsham of the north, whose descendants' banners yet fly. Today Kamau of the Oyo would join their ranks; today it was Kamau's turn to learn the grim lessons of war and sacrifice.

You will too, in your time.

It is not always so pleasant, growing up.

The boy looked east, towards unseen empires and wars of succession. He needed to return to his village and warn his mother and father.

"Come, Gyasi …

"We have much to do."

AFTERWORD

Approximately 1587
Village of the Oyo tribe, Kingdom of Benin (Western Africa)
A young warrior learns a harsh lesson on a morning patrol

War, until the 20th century, was not waged in order to kill all the combatants. The idea was to wound as many as possible, and in so doing to discourage the enemy … to get the other side to want to leave the battlefield.
This story is about the beginnings of such a war, a war of dissuasion.

This story comes from my screenplay version of my non-fiction book, *Teddy's Tantrum*. The book breaks down the aftermath of an incident in Teddy Roosevelt's administration. In 1906, President Roosevelt dismissed 167 members of the all-black 25th Infantry for a shoot-up in Texas. Sixty-five years later, a writer named John D. Weaver wrote a book about it and the Army exonerated the men of the 25th.

I felt that the incident was part of a much longer and broader story – the rise to honor of the black warrior. I believe the ancestors of the men of the 25th had also been patrolling borderlands against the empire's foes: this fictional story is my version of a prequel to the American warriors' story.

I have placed it in the western kingdoms of Benin because that is the region where so many of the eventual American slaves were captured – villages like the one of these young warriors were destined for slavery.

This story has no obvious role model, so it is possible I am beginning to break into some kind of original territory.

Benin sculpturesWikimedia Commons

HISTORICAL CONTEXT

My depiction of the elite Edo warrior is based on the Zulu, who once roamed the grasslands of Ghana and Mali in tightly disciplined bands.

"Several large political groupings emerged [in the early 1800's] to control the area between the Thukela and Black Mfolozi rivers. The Zulus ... were initially no more than subordinate allies to one of these groups, but their rising commenced with sometime between 1816 and 1818, when a minor son of the ruling chief
[ShakakaSenzangakhona] ... was raised up to control of the clan... by 1824, the Zulus had eclipsed all their rivals."

-- Ludwig Alberti in his book *Account of the Tribal Life and Customs of the Xhosa in 1807*.

Shaka, called by European historians the Napoleon of his day, trained an army so swift and savage that they "... shocked even the hardest professional soldiers ... who opposed them ..." according to Alberti. Once the main army was mobilized, its explicit objective was to 'eat up' the enemy. "The Zulu army was committed to the concept of aggressive action … [Shaka's] military philosophy … was always to attack whenever possible." As a result, the men of the African patrols were filled with tension. "The Zulu army in the field was like a spring that had been wound to breaking point by days of psychological preparation, and it required only the presence of the enemy for it to snap."

CHARACTERS

Kamau, the African boy is fresh, willing, delusionally self-confident, and almost fatally naïve. I modeled him on certain of my very young first-year cadets. They love the idea of war, and all the trappings of war, but when it comes to drawing blood there may be the shock of battle. In the end, Kamau rises to the occasion and manages to live up to the moment.

At first, he mistakenly pegs his kind commanding office (Kunle) for a boring teacher. When Kunle proves impossibly brave, it is too late to make amends. I tried to suggest in the ending that Kamau becomes the next great leader of his tribe. There may be a second story there.

The Edo warrior does Kamau and his village a great favor by keeping them away from the wars of succession. Farming villages like theirs would be swept up in bloody conflict and destroyed in such a war.

I have big plans for the lead character, Kamau, and his (seemingly) simple-minded sister. Their descendants join the mainstream of the Navigator saga at the moment one of the 'Colonials' figures stumbles into the 18th century Bedouin wars, in the north.

We study the Kingdoms of Kush far less than we do the Kingdoms of Charlemagne and Henry VIII. The Songs of Aksum are far less familiar to history students than the Song of Roland. Africa's is an emerging history. Scholars like Zeinab Badaw, Kwame Anthony Appiah and Henry Louis Gates are helping usher African civilizations into the light. Untold epics will one day make their way into our global narrative.

Anyone with an interest in African history is directed towards *The Fate of Africa: A History of the Continent*, by Martin Meredith and Toby Green's *A Fistful of Shells: West Africa.* Anything by Henry Louis Gates is worth reading.

AMSTERDAM

The Caliph's Gift

The Dutch Revolt, which began among a few thousand refugees in northwestern Europe, had spread until it affected millions of people and brought about the collapse of the greatest world empire ever seen ... There was fighting in Ceylon, Japan and Indonesia, in southern and western Africa, on the Indian, Pacific and Atlantic Oceans, and of course in Brazil and the Low Countries. It all stemmed from the revolt of the Netherlands. The struggle had become ... the First World War.

– Historian Geoffrey Parker

Artwork by Well-Bee

PART I: AN UNFAIR REQUEST

"*See it*, book-keep," said Pienaar.

"*Ecquis cursum inflectet*."

Well, I certainly did not see it, and if none may deflect its course, I would gladly step out of its way.

"It is not my problem," I stated, knowing this may well get me fired (even after two years on the job).

"This is one of Vondel's accounts. Sir."

It was a busy Friday morning. The unscrupulous head of the shipping agency which employed me, Master Peter Pienaar, stood before my work station.

He had one of his stubby arms on his hip, in his signature mock-jaunty pose; he enjoyed carrying himself as if he were the host of an ongoing party, and not the work-averse proprietor of a book-keeping sweatshop. Beside him stood that magnificent phony, Vondel. Vondel, head clerk and Pienaar's nephew, stood in the light of my window, his mop of blonde hair flopping over his high collar, a time piece hanging ridiculously from his neck, measuring the hours he was able to masquerade as a real clerk.

Beside him stood that magnificent phony, Vondel.

"Try to look at it not as a problem at all, Sykes, but an opportunity. For *all* of us."

Master Pienaar smiled in that tight, unhappy way that is not a smile at all. "An opportunity for our little firm to capture one of the great accounts of the day. Caliph Murad the IV, leader of the Ottoman Empire. No small fish, eh?"

This pair of pretenders had just asked me to drop all my other responsibilities and execute a complete ledger balance for the newly docked *Casimir*. In the next eight hours. This on a Friday, when I had capital journals due Monday for each of four VOC ships, as well as bills of lading for our largest Hanseatic client. Also due Monday. The tides were three days from perfect, and ships had to sail. While book-keeps may alter their schedules, nature does not. It was a massive amount of work.

"I care not a fig for Murad the Fourth," I declared. "I cannot, without abandoning our other clients."

"Come, come," said Pienaar with his fake jollity. "A nice challenge for you, what what?"

No no, I almost replied. I bit my lip.

I have a bad temper.

I have a bad temper, and I work hard to keep it in check. I never worked harder than at that moment, sitting at my work station, watching through the window as the pages played mumblety-peg on the green grass in the gardens, with these two smug idiots standing by my desk and grinning at me as they piled on me more work than any two other clerks in the shipping agency.

"Vondel should do it." I pushed the folder of documents back towards the pair. "It is he who will be presenting to the client."

And he is paid twice my wages for doing half the work, I refrained from adding.

"Well, that's certainly true, Matthias," tutted Pienaar. "Certainly true. I just wish I could spare him."

"Look, we have spent the greater part of a week dining on stinking eels and God-knows *horse*radish with the stinking Orientals in order to secure this client," said Vondel. "You must do your part."

As I saw it, I was doing *all* the parts.

Around me percolated the busy hubbub of the shipping agency Pineaar & Braudel. It was the summer of 1610, and it seemed like all the far-flung ports of the seven seas had sent us their cargoes at the same time. Amsterdam's docks and shallows were filled with all manner of fly-boats and galleons; English carracks of the Hawkins kind, with their forecastles removed; old-fashioned bilanders and Spanish nao; several fast corvettes and fluyts of every flag, size, shape, description and condition. The gargantuan *Zeeland* had just docked in the last hour, overflowing with bounty from a four-month Baltic voyage. As second clerk, I had the responsibility to assign teams of *boekholders* to inventory each and every vessel under contract to the firm; and if no reliable book-keep was available, to do it myself; and to sign each and every balanced ledger as true and complete. To all the merchants, all the owners, all the partners, all the sea captains and shareholders in all the ports that dotted the known oceans, my signature was bond.

Our offices and Master Pienaar's town-house shared a plot on the Beveland canal. Outside my window, beneath the blue sky, beyond the boys playing their knife games among flowers and vegetables in the garden, I could see rooftops, and the canals of Amsterdam, and beyond that a gleaming sliver of ocean. I longed to be done with all this. I longed to be at sea, with my late father, on a ship moving through blue waters, where city artifice and dread compromise falls away, and you measure your passage only by the stars.

"From where you sit, Matthias, you see only more paperwork," said Pienaar, growing impatient. "I understand that. But from where I sit, I see one of the most lucrative and prestigious clients this firm could hope for." Pienaar's lectures always include a warning about selfishness, and holding myself and my own comforts above the firm; they always ended with how lucky I was that he had hired me at all. "If he ever will sign the agreement. God knows. He is an odd bird, and seems only to circle, never to perch."

"Others vie for the Caliph's account," warned Vondel darkly. As if I cared.

Sunlight glinted off the pages' knife blades in the gardens. Sails moved in the distance. At heart, I am a cold person, and I calculated the best course of action for myself.

"It will be ready tomorrow morning," I said. "Seven o'clock"

* * *

Money flows to water.

Capital – accumulated money, that is, money to invest in enterprise, money that makes all things sprout and without which there is no school, no church, no commerce, no shipbuilding or ships – capital likes trade, and trade is one of the many benefits waters bring.

Money flows to water, and all waters lead to Rotterdam. All the world's water trade routes come together in the Dutch nation.

By a series of flukes, the Dutch dominated sea trade at that moment. Two generations earlier, when the Hapsburgs had asked the Protestants and Jews to leave certain cities like Antwerp and Bruges and Ghent, they had all come to the Netherlands. These were skilled tradesmen, ministers, lawyers, broad-thinking scholars and mathematicians and merchants, large and small. Almost the entire elites of Flanders and Brabant were transplanted to the Low Countries, along with Sephardic Jews and Huguenots from France. Then a storm broke the wall of the Zeeland lake, and suddenly the North Sea had a connection to the Rhine, and the network of rivers serving the vast German interior. It was a convergence of north-south trade routes with east-west: a global nexus.

The families of the Low Countries saw the possibilities. The Dutch East India Company, or *Verenigde Oostindische Compagnie* (VOC) was formed as the vessel of their ambitions to send ships scurrying to and fro along the meridians, to ferry New World good to the rest of the world. To dominate world trade. The Bank of Amsterdam was formed to fund the VOC. The clever Dutch applied a crankshaft to a windmill and invented the sawmill so they could build the most efficient crafts to sail the seven seas. Dutch shipyards produced almost the entire German fleet, and half of France's.

Now two empires dominated the globe: Spain in the west and the Ottomans in the East. The Ottomans, watching colonial empires being collected by tiny seagoing nations like ours, wanted in on the game. They had been on the sidelines, collecting transit fees while the merchant fleets robbed the Orient and Afrique. Now Caliph Murad – influenced, many said, by his smart, Western-savvy Vizier, Sokollu -- began to think of himself as European, and turned his attention westwards. That meant rivalry in all ways with Spain – a sprawling, smart, talented people who woke up every morning believing it was their destiny to rule all others.

Now Caliph Murad began to think of himself as European, and turned his attention westwards.

So it was only natural that the Ottomans -- Caliph Murad the Fourth, that is – sought us out an ally against Spain. It was this partnership that Pienaar and Vondel negotiated, as representatives of the VOC. The Dutch merchant force wished to cut ever deeper into the Oriental world.

My skiff turned sharply round the vast stern of the *Wijnstock*. My little boat moved briskly among the great vessels, like a robin gliding among giant trees.

I was headed towards the Maashaven piers, where *Casimir* lay at anchor. The draft is twenty-four meters there, enough for the deepest keels.

My left leg is lame. I prefer to use a well-worn little skiff to move about Rotterdam's canals rather than walking its wooden bridges and cobbled streets.

I needed to first inventory the *Casimir's* cargo and cross-check it with the receiving merchants' contracts. The bills of lading were next, and then the Captain's log. I was lucky in that the records had been kept by an apparently fastidious Croatian, who wrote plainly, kept clean columns, and recorded every possible factor in his narratives (including weather). Lastly, I needed to create the capital ledger, calculating each seaman's and officer's and investing partner's share, for a ten-month voyage like that of the *Casimir* represented over two million florins in worth.

It was a sunny morning. Gulls glided and called out above me. As I passed close to the hulls, I could see how each had weathered her voyage; crewman and shipyard teams swarmed on ladders and nets and ropes over the hulls and decks, scrubbing, making repairs, mending sails. Tillers had been removed, their component parts laid up on sawhorses. I saw flags being steam-cleaned, officers' linens aired out, pilots and navigators poring over maps and ledger books. My skiff caught a breeze in her little sail and surged along the tall keel of the *Van Rooyen*. I sat on the gunwale and leaned back. An iron worker recognized me and called my name. I waved.

I saw the *Casimir* looming ahead.

"Well, Matty, let's get 'em down," said Jonker, who was guarding the pier that morning and knew me well. "I'll climb up the ladders and hand 'em down. How does that sound?"

"You are a good man," said I.

I unwrapped a pan of brisket and fresh bread and gravy and vegetables which I had brought from Pienaar's kitchen for him and the elderly drunkard Mickler, a respected navigator in his younger years who now spent his days on the docks. The men of the piers appreciate their food.

As we boarded the *Casimir* and showed our papers, three crewmen – Gunderman, by their dialect – jibed at me. "Who is it that walks with a cane, like an old man?" commented the one furthest away, imitating my slow gait. I stopped and turned, hoping he would come close enough; it had been too long a day to accept another insult.

"Come, Matty -- " Johannes Mickler, showing insight through his drunkenness, took my arm. We made our way to the cargo holds.

Within ten minutes, I found why Pienaar had wanted me, and not Vondel, to take this assignment.

It was sunset by the time we finished.

We emerged into a balmy evening.

The *Casimir* rocked gently among the shoulders of her sister ships, her mast and spars casting sharp shadows in the slanting sunlight. Having found food for the day, the white birds tucked in and cleaned their feathers, done for the day. The tide would soon be cresting, bringing all Neptune's bounty and mystery up and in; then the tidal window would quickly close. I had much work to do before morning. I said my goodbyes to Jonker and old Mickler.

One of the Gundermen tried to trip me as I debarked.

I grabbed his throat and choked him, not letting go even when his eyes went white. Just as his body started to go slack, I smashed my cane's head into his face three times, fiercely, for his earlier remark had put me in a dark mood, and my anger rushed back in an instant. He fell to the ground, bloody and crying and gasping for breath. I invited his friends in their own rough tongue to come get more, if they cared to.

My skiff creaked and leapt in the water, eager for the evening breezes.

The sail home was pleasant.

PART II: I MEET THE VIZIER SOKOLLU

On the next morning, the rising sun found me sleeping heavily. Sea chanties serenaded me in my dreams.

I had left the vetted *Casimir* documents at my desk, with comments so well-detailed that even Vondel could make a clear report.

I was dreaming about that particular passage of the Bosphorus when you are suspended between the Aegean behind and the Black Sea ahead, with an inexplicable view of the Topkapi palace on the leeward, and my father was calling my name to come and look at the dolphins when Marta, one of the pages, awoke me.

"Master Sykes!"

She was shaking me. A thrill of danger was in her voice.

"Wake up! Please!"

"What time is it?" I asked groggily, still seeing Constantinople.

"Ten o'clock. Master Pienaar has sent an escort for you."

Escort -- ?

I was dimly aware of others standing, waiting in my close little chamber.

"The Caliph!" Marta was saying. "It is urgent -- "

* * *

Vizier Sokollu, grand minister to Murad the Fourth, Caliph of the Ottoman Empire, held up his hand to cease the discussions, which centered on the status of Dutch privateers under the proposed Ottoman treaty.

"Ah. Young Master Sykes," said Sokollu. "There you are."

I was seated along with a dozen advisors and lesser ministers at a long table in the formal room. The floor was checkerboard tiles. Drapes and pillows and servants and candles of incense decorated the chamber's perimeters, in the Oriental fashion. Sokollu was a solidly built man, formidable, smart, with watchful eyes and a resonant voice. He was a man with a physical presence, and he made a point of rising from his seat, surprisingly lithe for a man of his bulk, and walking towards me. I could tell from the way he walked that he had taken men's lives.

"We had a query. Regarding the ledger accounts of the *Casimir*."

Of course. This was why Pienaar and Vondel had positioned me between the Casimir accounts and themselves. They had known, or suspected, of the irregularities, and did not wish to be explaining them to the Vizier. They wanted distance from that unpleasantness.

"The ledger accounts were … *skewed*, I understand," said Sokollu, clearly displeased. He held my report in his hand, but he wanted to hear it from me.

"Aye."

"It was a rich cargo. One of the richest I have seen."

"Not for you, sire," said I. "Not as it was previously recorded." He stood directly across from me now. "There are four account books on such a voyage, Learned One: a memorial; a journal; a debts ledger; and a participants' book, or subscription ledger. Of these, the last is the most significant. What you saw was the memorial ledger. It shows you a sliver of the transaction, but sadly not the entirety."

"I see," replied the Vizier.

"The memorial ledger does not include details of capital payments. Transfers. Tolls. Carrying costs. Handling fees. A capital ledger *does* include such details. In the *Casimir's* case," I continued, "the subscription ledger showed us that the stevedores were directed to place all the valuable cargo in the subscription holds, and all of the least valuable cargo in the client's holds. Your holds."

"And how much was the discrepancy?" he demanded.

"Two hundred twenty thousand florins."

The assembled men drew their breath at the figure.

"Is that legal?"

"If the client agrees to it, by signing the bills of lading. As you apparently did. As a result, the subscribers – the ship's partners -- can claim a commission on the superior cargo, leaving you the lesser-valued cargo. Iberian wheat, Baltic herring, and so on. Iberian wheat, while most excellent, fetches one-twentieth the price, by weight, as does Mallorcan pepper."

"And this has been corrected?"

"Yes."

"Overnight? You intercepted the shipments—"

"All of them," bragged Vondel. "And recombined the cargoes. As I told you just now."

"Not a single peppercorn was ever brought to market," chimed in Pienaar. "You will regain your entire proper share, sire."

Sokollu looked at me.

"It has been a busy night," I said.

The medieval merchants formed simple partnerships, and Pacioli's system satisfied their limited appetite for precision. Today we have 16 or 20 partners on a single voyage lasting two years, and seaman's shares, and bankers, and insurers, and agency fees, and discounts for weather, and tables to calculate profits and losses to the capital accounts. We require stricter observances.

"Know ye the captain of the *Casimir*?" asked Sokollu.

"My lord, it matters not whether the captain of the *Casimir* is Henry the Navigator or Pope Marcellus the Second." I was exhausted, and no matter what I did, Vondel would take credit. "The figures tell the story, my lord. Perhaps it was by accident," I added, as a sort of face-saving gesture.

Every accounting every reckoning is a puzzle to solve. Balancing a ledger is a face-to-face encounter with a job that has been performed: has it been performed properly? Through the document, the way each entry is recorded, the handwriting itself, the words chosen for the narratives, you quickly begin to see the person behind it. Above all, you see his thinking: does he intend to clarify, or to conceal? To make an accounting professional or make it obscure? Everything about the *Casimir* – not just the lading documents and ledgers, but the arrangement of the inventory, the labeling of the cargo, the shape and contours of the shelving, the division of the holds, everything -- told you that the intent was to conceal. I knew within minutes that corrections would be in order, and where I might look to find them.

"But I supervised the ledger entries myself," insisted Sokollu. "With the Croatian."

"Keep your Caliph's job then," I answered honestly, "for there is little future for you as a book-keep."

For a moment, the chamber hesitated. Sokollu stopped in his pacing, to turn and face me. I made it a point to ignore him. He laughed and nodded and clapped his hands in pleasure.

"Yes, I think I *will* keep my Caliph's job, Dutchman. Thank you for the career advice. But why did we not catch this … irregularity? And such a costly one at that …"

"There is no cost at all," Piennaar was quick to clarify. "For we – as your agents -- have done our duty, and corrected the error."

"Sykes corrected it, not you – " observed the Vizier.

"Caliph, your system is Paciolian," said I. "It is *medieval*. It is not meant for such transactions. It cannot reflect the true value of such a ship's inventory."

"And yours does?"

"To the last grain of wheat. To the last kernel of corn."

"After adjustments, it is well reconciled," said Vondel weakly, twirling his beaded necklace. "A most profitable voyage."

Seeming satisfied on the subject, Sokollu clapped his hands and waved his servants to bring in a new round of refreshments. The *devshirmeh* brought platters of assorted viands and fruit, and pitchers of water and wine.

* * *

"Now," said Sokollu in a changed, grave tone. "On the larger topic of the treaty. Between our two nations."

Instantly the room was silenced. It was as if all the air in the room had condensed, freezing us each in position.

"Can we hear what young Master Sykes thinks?" Sokollu asked.

"Can we hear what young Master Sykes thinks?" Sokollu asked.

Vondel choked on the fig in his mouth (he was always eating). All eyes turned to me.

"My first assistant may answer that more prettily, Vizier," said Pienaar.

"None the less."

A chair creaked. No one dared move.

"Sykes is the least pious of clerks, sire – " protested Pienaar.

"It is not piety I seek," insisted Sokollu. He gestured for me to speak.

I looked hard at Pienaar. His brows rose. He squirmed. He cocked his head in question. Then he seemed to relent, and nodded once to me.

There are moments – I am sure you have known them yourself -- in the course of human events that seem to slow down. You can almost hear a page being raised from the book of your life, about to turn a new chapter: so it was here. I had been commanded to attend this absurd conference; it had nothing to do with me, and I had no interest one way or another. Yet I had been thrust squarely in the middle of a dilemma fraught with hidden meanings and trap doors, none of my own making; and my own fate suddenly hung in the balance. There is no preparation for such moments. They are coming, reader, always coming and never announced.

"You are familiar with the treaty, Sykes?"

"Not as much as Master Vondel," I said, hoping to slip out of the noose.

"Give me your honest opinion, young Sykes. Should I sign it? Will the Caliph behead me in six months' time? Are there hidden dangers in it that I cannot see? Answer as if you were my own advisor." Seeing my hesitancy, he leaned towards me and lowered his voice, as if he and I were alone. "Fear not."

The brave die only once, I told myself.

"If I were the Caliph, it is the sixth and seventh standards I would amend. Those are the most important, in the end. Take a commission on the commerce in these ports," I rose in my chair and pointed to the flat maps of the Mediterranean, "and not a flat fee. The trade routes are worth double what you think they are, for the Gruyen shipyards even now build fluyts with twice the capacity. These larger ships would surpass the standards within eighteen months, and this agreement is six years in length. You see how they would carry far more value per cubic rood. The present formula does not take that into account."

"Ah," said Sokollu, nodding in understanding.

"Outlaw the private tugs and barges. Nationalize them, so that the agencies of the Caliph are licensed to navigate the Straits, and none other. The barges charge too much for the time and too little for the navigation."

The Dutch East India Company insignia

"Legitimize the Dutch privateers. They do your work for you, with no cost to assemble a navy. You can follow the existing Amsterdam guidelines for the licenses."

"You say I should nationalize the ports. Yet the Ottoman staff is not up to the task. There is corruption and nepotism. The *bakshis* are well-known to err in their own favor. This will not do: merchants cannot also be regulators. I do not possess honest regulators."

"No, you do not," I replied.

He smoothed the pages of the unsigned agreement, indicating that he awaited my clarification.

"Hire our firm as your consultants. For a year, we will supervise all the Caliph's ports, and train Turks in our system. Master Pienaar and his partners are known around the world as honest traders. Between them, they have trained men who sail in hundreds of merchant vessels, men who would welcome it."

"Dutchmen regulating the Ottoman ports," mused Sokollu. "It is quite a picture."

"It will give comfort to all. What you may lose in favor of your concessionaires, you will gain in commission. The Caliph will hold full sway over the commerce of a dozen ports. In truth, not merely in title."

By its murmur and nodded heads, the assemblage at the long table assented to the truth of this prediction.

"How *does* your mind work, clerk?" asked Sokollu.

"I have said too much," I replied, bowing my head slightly, knowing I had told the truth and, in doing so, had lost all chance of advancement in this fickle world.

I had told the truth and, in doing so, had lost all chance of advancement in this fickle world.

"Master Sykes. Given these points you mention, would you sign this treaty?" asked Sokollu at length.

"Aye," I replied. "I would. It is to your advantage in every way."

"Very well," said Sokollu, and in saying that he meant, "*The matter is settled*."

He motioned for the documents to be brought before him.

Accompanied by a round of applause from the surprised gathering, he signed three copies of the agreement. He passed them to Master Pienaar, who signed with a flourish. The commissions on the first month alone would pay our staff for the year. The *devshirmeh*, the Caliph's Christian conscripts, scampered to and fro while the Turk scribes applied blotting pads and official seals to the documents.

Yet in this success, I had chosen ruin. I had violated the chain of authority. No second clerk speaks as I had spoken, only partners. No matter the outcome, I would have to be punished, for the guild members protect the established order as they protect their lives.

PART III: PUNISHMENT AND AN UNEXPECTED OFFER

I had never seen Pienaar so mad.

"I would fire you altogether were the damned Vizier not so smitten with you." His hands shook as he signed the documents Vondel held for him.

His voice was cold with fury.

"By your actions, *Matthias,* you have extended your term of service. My smart young man. Extended your term of service *and* lowered your own wages. That is what all your cleverness has earned -- "

"You can't do that," said I. "There is no just cause -- "

"It is already done. And you need to re-read your letters of apprenticeships if you think there is no just cause." He looked only at Vondel, as if I were not present. "Here is my letter to Master Sombart. Vondel, please witness and stamp it, so we may send it off to the Board of Registrars at once."

The Registry would never take my side over Pienaar.

For my good efforts, I had just lost a year and a half of my life. I had added eighteen months of servitude to Pienaar. Before I would earn my license.

* * *

Soon the tides fell, and with them my spirit. We watched the ships' stately progress into the Atlantic's vanishing point; with them, I felt, vanished all my hopes. Dark thoughts engulfed me. All the evils of past times -- wrongs done to me and, worse, the bitter mistakes of my own making -- revisited me, waking and sleeping.

Pienaar and another partner departed for Flanders, to visit a series of subscribers, taking Vondel in tow. I was left to do all my work and theirs as well. But few ships came into Amsterdam's wharves in a low tide such as that.

I joined the pages in their knife games, in the garden. Marta made me use my left hand. She said I was too good at throwing.

I spent time with Jonkler and old Johannes Mickler, punting among the northern docks. Mickler, when he was sober, told us long accounts of the ancient navigators, and of Fieschi, Colom's pilot on the second voyage, who was rumored to have found treasure off the coast of Africa. We spent a day at the Lelystad shipyards, watching the construction of the new man-o-war *De Zeven Provinciën*, its wooden ribcage resting at an angle like a great skeleton.

I visited five of the seven other shipping agencies, inquiring for openings. There were none. Pienaar had poisoned the well against me, no doubt telling all the firms that I could not be trusted. I was trapped. I could not shake the dark cloud that had fallen over me. All my good work and careful planning – gone, in one uncontrolled moment. I could see no light ahead. I was worse off than ever. *Would it ever be thus?* I well knew the answer: *Yes.*

I was surprised one morning to hear Marta calling my name. I could hear concern in the tone of her voice. I walked into the receiving room to see a pair of the Ottoman guards, which some call janissaries, waiting for me.

"The Vizier requests an audience," said one, in excellent Dutch. "He departs tomorrow, and wishes to review the next steps in the account." They insisted that I attend.

We arrived in the embassy to find the Vizier seated in his offices. He stood as I entered; there were no formalities this time, for we were working partners.

A slim, flat, decorated case was laid on the table before him. He slid it across to me.

"A gift. I wish to thank you," he said, smiling. "And to lure you."

I opened the lid to reveal two pairs of *kilij*, the thin-bladed Turkish throwing daggers. The scabbards and hilts were each decorated in the same design as the inlaid trunks, with intricate spiny margins and showy spikes; yet these were no jewel-hilted ornaments, but a soldier's weapons. I picked up one of the dirks: it was weighted perfectly, balancing easily on my finger.

"I – I … It is … A thousand thanks, nazir." To refuse such a gift would be a great insult. "The Vizier is beyond generous."

"You will find them well balanced," he said. "More than pretty presents."

"The glyphs which decorate the stocks," said I. "Do they carry a meaning?"

"Yes. These are part of the *Yataghan*. It is an ancient tablet which prophesies the coming of the Third Lord of Night. He signals an epic fight between good and evil. One to consume the worlds known and unknown. Let us hope the prophecies are wrong.

"May the gods smile on all of us," he added, and then, as though merely mentioning a passing thought, he added:

"Your father was captain of the *Tobias*, was he not?"

It was my turn to show surprise.

"A good sailor is known in all ports," shrugged Sokollu. "He was killed at Simancas, in the encounter with the Spanish Duke of Kathgor, if I am not mistaken …"

He gestured for his servants to leave the chamber. When we were alone, he lay down an intricate map of his home nation.

"We are not so different, we two. Orphans who make their own fates."

He spread the Ottoman map on the table and squared it.

"*Sykes*," he said, and from the tone of his voice, and the way he moved his thick hand across the map, I knew we had entered an entirely different realm of conversation.

"See here."

He pointed to the map, to a region and well away from Constantinople.

"My people are the Oirates, descended from the Telengetes of the Altai."

"The Caliph and I descend from different tribes. Tribes that may soon be at war with one another."

He removed an envelope from his pocket and slid it across to me.

"I would like to hire you, Matthias. This is a contract. Between me and you.

"A thousand florins each month, for fourteen months. Renewable at a slightly higher rate."

I saw from the frank expression and his forward posture, already looking and speaking ahead, that he was in earnest.

"At this moment, we – the Oirates, that is, my own tribe – are declaring our independence from the Ottoman Empire.

"It will be an armed rebellion. We should already control the ports of Selanik and Izmit. They are two of the most lucrative in the empire. We also control the lower Murmansk, as you may know. The only passage between Gallipoli and the Dardenelles. Quite a lucrative franchise, if handled properly.

"I have just now sent a letter by courier, officially resigning from the Caliph's service and taking over as Governor of the Oirates. We are a new and independent state, with a fleet of fifty-two ships. We will need wise counsel in our maritime affairs.

"It will be an armed rebellion. We should already control the ports of Selanik and Izmit."

"I do not mean Pienaar's firm," he said. "I mean yours."

"But I have no firm, sire -- "

"You do now.

"A deposit of three thousand florins has been left in the Registry Office, with the Spaniard, Sarmiento. I believe him to be as honest and as discreet as you, Matthias.

"The statutes require a water board member to be signatory. You may know one or two."

Old Mickler? But how would Sokollu know about him --?

"The rewards are great, Matthias. You would in a single day own one of the significant shipping agencies. But so, too, are the risks. Spain will be against us"

I had not even considered that, but he was right: Philip was the Caliph's ally, so any enemy of the Ottoman Caliph was instantly an enemy of Spain … and Spain had agents all over the globe. Spain was the wrong enemy to make.

I did not give him an answer. Young men are flush almost to the point of madness with confidence, and ambition; but not so much that they cannot see glints of their own ruin.

"I will have an answer for you tomorrow morning," I told him.

"Take care," he warned. "Even now, word may be out."

He shook my hand with both of his, in the Western manner. I bowed, as best I could, and touched my forehead in the Oriental fashion. Sokollu smiled. His hands were powerful, his speech plain and clear, and his smile genuine: this would be a good companion, a man to set sail with.

PART IV: A LITTLE BOAT RIDE

The skiff liked this section of the waters. Narrow and calm …

I was sailing upriver to clear my mind.

I took the dhow, barely larger than a catboat, and set out east on the canals, and then north.

It was a warm evening. A light wind blew from the northwest, and avenues of trees lined the canal, perfuming the air. I reckoned rain would arrive soon from a line of dark clouds I could see gathering along the western horizon. The boat had no cargo but me and no draft, and I could float above sandbars and debris as I pleased: we sailed through rich marshy pastures, past low-eaved, reed-thatched farms. Black and white cows standing in sight of the water watched my progress. Time slowed. My thoughts spread out.

Spain would oppose Sokollu and the Oirates. If I were noticed at all, Philip would as soon crush me if he thought I supported the Oirates cause. And I intended just that. Already I had jotted down templates for revenues and tariffs along the southern Sea of Murmansk, and sketched the seal of the new nation to stamp on my documents.

I passed under the bridge at Tholen.

I had first thought book-keeping was a skill. Then I believed it to be a discipline. Now I believe it to be a way of life, for I know that a man's method of accounting comes from deep within – from a life lived a certain way. A Borneo man will devise his own way of counting his poultry, and it would be different from the system a Chinese man devises, for they see the world very differently. Double-entry book keeping is something only a Dutchman could conceive of (although an Englishman is the first to recognize its worth and adopt it, and a German is second). It satisfies concerns that a Dutchman would have. It makes sense in his world.

Arabic book-keeping can be wonderfully descriptive, and precise to the Nth degree, and even deeply meaningful, but only to the man who recorded it (and perhaps his cousins). It is idiosyncratic. It is personal; each book-keep has his or her own system of notations and references. Therefore, as any kind of universal standard, it is useless. Turkish book-keeping is double-entry, yet while it requires transactions to be recorded as opposing debit and credits, it does not tell the entire story of the transactions. It does not distinguish between the owner's financial interests and the firm's interest. It does not account for common monetary value. It is not *systematic.* The Dutch system is comprehensive. You may objectively determine whether you are earning the optimal return on your investment.

In this system of banking, there was a deep need for honest book-keeping. The importance of reliable records pointed to where my future lay … I had already picked up the basics of navigation, and collected enough pilot's books to know a thing or two. With a *boekholder's* license, I would be a man of value in any port on any sea. And here a license was more or less being given to me.

Sokollu was right. Johannes had official status. He could start a new shipping firm as lead partner – and I as managing partner -- and together we could open accounts and do business in any port. My new firm would have all the rights and responsibilities of any shipping agent. Pienaar and all his gossip could not stop me.

But there would be no turning back. If the Oirates faltered, my fate would follow theirs. However, if I could muster business independent of theirs, perhaps shift to another port, my new firm would be launched, with clientele of its own.

The sun set as I jibed onto the *Issjel*, followed that stream, and passed the village of Zupthen. This had been the scene of an infamous massacre under the Spanish Inquisition. Bodies had hung from the branches that now caught the warm sunlight. We passed a Frisian punt.

My mind was made up.

I steered for home.

The stars were out by the time I approached the little dock near our offices. I would have to clear all my belongings quickly, and tell no one. I imagined Pienaar's smug face when he heard the news.

I saw three figures ahead, under the lamps of the dock. Three attackers and one victim, in the shadows between two boats.

I recognized their victim from his croaking voice: it was Vondel.

They did not imagine me gliding towards them, nor did they hear anything, for I approached from the windward.

I lifted one of the hooked spars from beneath the gunwale and hefted it as my skiff slid alongside the dock.

One assassin I struck in the back with my dagger as I approached. None noticed him fall.

I was able to sweep the legs of the other two out from under them before they realized I was there.

I grabbed Vondel and toppled him into my skiff. One of the attackers lunged. I threw the spar at him but my leg buckled as I threw, and I missed.

He lunged --

A gust of wind carried us away sharply, so that he missed us.

"Sykes!" cried Vondel as our sail filled and we skimmed out of danger. "If this is to be my last moment on this plane, let me die begging your forgiveness. I have acted most pridefully towards you, and unfairly. I cannot enter the Realms of Heaven without -- "

"You're not going to die," said I.

"I'm not?"

"No. Just shut up for a moment."

"Say you forgive me, Sykes. I need to know -- "

"I forgive you."

"How could you? I have been monstrous – "

"You must stop the bleeding, Vondel. Squeeze hard. There. That's it. They didn't hit anything important -- "

"Important? I am in AGONY, Sykes –

"But **why**" – Vondel moaned. "What did I *do* –"

"They thought you were me," I told him.

"But – who … Ye GODS! That HURTS! Wh –what could cause such behavior --"

"Here we go. Watch your head."

"They kept asking me about the Dardenelles. Passage in the Oirates. What does that mean, Sykes?"

"There is civil war among the Ottomans," I answered.

Vondel considered this for a moment. Imagining a world that did not revolve around himself was new to him.

"Ah. I see," he concluded at some length.

"We are in deep waters now, Sykes."

Reflections of the giddy stars and solemn moon shone on the canal.

I thought I heard sea chanties floating on the waters, from the bay, beyond the docks, but I hear those in my dreams, too, so I cannot say in certainty.

* * *

The next morning, just after dawn, I arrived at the embassy to find Vizier Sokollu gone.

"Pressing matters have called him home," the janissary told me. "The *Vrede* departs within the hour.

One of our messengers, young Marta, handed me a letter.

"He left this for you."

Only three words graced the paper:

Ecquis cursum inflectet.

I made my way to the docks where the Vrede lay.

It had begun to rain.

From the docks, I scanned the quarterdeck of the square-rigged flute as the Turks set sail. A burly figure at the rail, wrapped in a dark cloak, saw me and gave a small wave of his right hand.

Marta waved back.

I saw that Vizier Sokollu was well protected by his loyal guard. Well he understood the stakes.

None may deflect its course.

He had known I would accept his offer.

The adventure had begun. My heart raced.

I turned to walk homewards, through the wharf's alleyways. My mind was swimming with thoughts. There was so much to do: I must appear before the syndicate, to discuss with the Amsterdam families the terms and timeline of our treaty. All the privateers needed to be re-mapped and reassigned, subtracting certain Mediterranean routes and recommissioning those who preyed on the Ottoman – should I say Oirates -- cargoes. I needed to write the papers for the partnership. We would need to hire new clerks.

At the edge of my senses, I heard a shrill whistle –

I dropped to the ground.

A blade clattered above me.

I heard a quick hollow sound, feet rushing on the quay --

I turned to glimpse the assassin's gleaming eyes and a second knife in his hand; a moment later two *kilij* daggers had pinned his throat to the staves of a barrel.

I had hurled them flat and head-high with all my might, but I could not be sure how they struck. I clambered across the wooden dock as fast as I could with my accursed leg, holding my little pocket-knife at the ready and looking for a second attacker, but none came.

They had sent a lone killer to eliminate the lame cleric: it was a mistake they would not make again.

I yanked the daggers out of the man's throat.

He fell heavily onto the dock.

He flayed on his back like a fish, frantically gasping and choking on his own blood. I tried to calm him.

I could see that he was young -- younger than I -- a thin deadly boy with narrow features and delicate hands.

I cushioned his head with my jacket, but I could not staunch the free flow of blood. I spoke to him in one language, then a second, and finally a third, which he recognized.

"May God accept your soul," I said in that language. "Who sent this warrior to kill me?" I asked.

"*The Abaddon*," he whispered. "They will send others."

He had been sent from the New World to murder me, having nothing to do with the Ottoman Turks or their treaties or the rebel Oirates, but everything to do with me, and my father, and my role in the approaching battle. It was part of a scheme I was only beginning to understand.

He gripped my shoulder. Light fluttered in those dying eyes. "Oh! I hear them!" He looked up at me. "My mother … ah, I -- I cannot -- *ugh*!"

I leaned close. Gurgling and coughing, he told me his name and his town. I promised to send word to his kin, and to say that he had died bravely.

Marta appeared from the shadows, pale-faced, shaken by the sight of so much blood. It was her warning that had saved my life.

"Will he die, Matthias?"

"Yes. We are at war now."

We waited there, in the rain. The assassin's breathing grew labored, then he shivered and fell still. Marta started to cry.

I stood over the dead body. Raindrops fell on the wooden surface of the wharf with tiny, almost silent splashes.

I left one of my daggers sticking point-down in the plank beside the assassin's body, as a message. Philip, King of Castile, Count of Barcelona, Marques of the Holy Roman Empire, would know that it was Matthias Sykes, cleric, son of Jonathan Sykes, a mighty navigator and proud father, who had sent his minion to the nether regions.

"What tongue was that you spoke to him?" asked Marta.

"Hungarian," I answered.

Now the wheel had turned. Death joined destiny in chasing me from my comfortable candle-lit alcove.

None may deflect its course.

I gripped the hilt of the Caliph's gift, my fingers closing on the prophecies inscribed there. If no others appeared to oppose the savage coming of this Lord of Night, as he rose shambling and dripping and terrible from the seas, then I would do it alone.

If no others appeared to oppose the savage coming of this Lord of Night, then I would do it alone.

I swung Marta onto my back and turned for home.
Rain fell. Thunder sounded from the west. The storm was coming.

AFTERWORD

Amsterdam (1621)
Prelude to the Dutch Rebellion

The full-text version of this is still a little talky. I think I did begin – a little – to break into original territory here. The problem is that whatever conflict I have going, it is still too subtle for the reader, too deeply buried in the action and in long sections of dead prose (my specialty). I don't know why I see things this way; readers hate this.

In the most recent draft, I have tried to bring out the conflicts, and give them more shape. I have also tried to strengthen the arc of the story, so it doesn't read like the first chapter of a much longer work, which it is. There should be action sooner in the plot timeline. Once again, as one of my cadets pointed out in a course assessment, I am too clever for my own good (that is, not clever at all). Working on it.

CHARACTERS
Matthias, a sullen apprentice clerk, is mature for his age (17), for he has been to sea. An eventful 18-month voyage aboard the *Janzoon* to Batavia and back has left Matty Sykes fatherless, lame in one leg, and deeply suspicious of others' motives. Yet when a most unusual opportunity arises, Matthias finds that his sorry lot in life can change.

Matthias, I think, is a seaman first and a clerk second. He should probably be a navigator, but I could not make that work with this plot. I had a scene where he confronts his mysterious older brother, now a pirate, but luckily for you I omitted it, since it just clogged up my clean storyline. I say "clean" ironically. Marta does not survive the next plot cycle. Soon after his encounter with Sokollu, Matthias visits Johannes Mickler, an alcoholic former navigator with a shipping agent's license, and the firm Mickler, Sykes is born.

* * *

Two decades ago, I ran across a dissertation about the history of accounting, in which the author said this:

> Momentous developments in the prevailing accounting paradigm occur infrequently, which means that such transformations are highly significant events …One such significant conjuncture occurred in the late 16th and early 17th centuries when Paciolian

double-entry bookkeeping was transformed into the capitalistic form of double-entry bookkeeping.

-- *Capitalism and Accounting in the Dutch East India Company 1602-1923*, Jeffrey Stephen Robertson

I decided I would try to tell the story of the Dutch rebellion and the global conflict it ignited through the eyes of a shipping clerk. A book-keeper would have a most surprising view of the engine behind this dramatic global war, "the first world war." This idea proved to be a powerful one whose execution has gone wandering terribly off-course this past decade.

Binenhof 1651 by Van Bassen

The 17th century Dutch Revolt against Spanish tyranny – the true First World War, one historian calls it -- is alluring to me, and I spent two years in my 40's blocking out a vast story taking place against this backdrop.

This wonderful illustrator (pen-name: Wellbee) gave so much extra to this adaptation – split panels and a wealth of cinematic angles. I hope you get the chance to see his work online, where the lines are more visible.

* * *

The Caliph's Gift is really the opening sequence in a story cycle of the Dutch Revolt, the beginnings of the maritime firm that will channel the Navigators' resources and oppose the Spaniards. These events come just after those in *King James' Seventh Company* and feature two characters from that story.

The Dutch Revolt, which began among a few thousand refugees in north-western Europe, had spread until it affected millions of people and brought about the collapse of the greatest world empire ever seen ... There was fighting in Ceylon, Japan and Indonesia, in southern and western Africa, on the Indian, Pacific and Atlantic Oceans, and of course in Brazil and the Low Countries. It all stemmed from the revolt of the Netherlands. The struggle had become ... the First World War.

-- *Historian Geoffrey Parker*

One problem in tackling that scenario will be to depict the Spaniards in a more rounded way, since they have received several centuries of bad press. There is a richer story beneath the traditional premise of Emperor Phillip and the Evil Castilian Dukes versus the Free Men of the Tiny Seven Provinces.

You can't really tell yet, but I really like the Matthias character a lot. He reminds me of my son. Matthias is a central figure in the whole Navigators' saga, the founder of the shipping agency which is a common thread in all the stories.

EGIPTO

ARAB

FED

PRESTE IOAÕ

YES ?

Saloon Reunion

"Did you read 'em from the book?"
"No. I jes' showed them the pictures ..."

-- *Cherokee Trail*

Art by Boell Oyino
Color by Javelin Studio

"TAKE A WALK WITH US, PRETTY Miss."

Big Luke Rynert laughed too loudly.

"You look like you need some air."

The saloon suddenly grew quiet, for the words did not at all mean what they said.

It was one of those big, familiar rooms used for all manner of congregations, from dining to weddings to worship to community debate.

McCormack had invented a reaper. Science struck farming, and an explosion of productivity followed, for with McCormack's reaper one man could farm like six men. The land yielded geometrically more wheat than ever thought possible, a welcome multiplier at a time when all Europe's cities demanded bread. The rich soils of the California territories beckoned. Wagon trains of Grangers migrating into the bountiful western lands found cattlemen sitting on the best land, for the same soil that grew wheat and corn also grew green grass, grass to make cows grow fat (and highly profitable). Who owned the land? For a time, whoever could keep it.

Now this sad-eyed Granger girl looked at the big man sitting next to her at the breakfast table. The man had frozen: it was as if he were trying not to move, not even to breathe, so he would not attract attention. With a painful slowness, the girl's eyes looked up at the four gunmen surrounding the farmers' table. She was young – no more than sixteen – and there was defiance in her posture. But four men with guns were too many.

"Let's see what's under her *skirt*, Luke," leered one of the gunmen.

The long, cold-metal barrel of a Ballard rifle advanced towards her.

She closed her eyes; sudden tears formed, darkening her lashes, and Luke Rynert chuckled to see it.

One of Rynert's henchmen reached out to take hold of the fabric of the girl's dress --

A hand grabbed the gunman by the hair and flung him violently downward.

His bloody face ricocheted off the table. As if in slow motion, he fell backwards and landed skull-first with a sickening thud on the saloon's wooden floor.

Heads turned to see a lean, wolfish boy standing among the breakfast tables.

"Your friend seemed kinda edgy, Rynert."

His voice was cold, yet the words were uttered with emphasis, as if they were coded, or part of an ancient script, or as if only he and one or two others could know their full meaning.

Big Luke Rynert peered at the blue eyes under the flat-brimmed hat.

"Ain't your fight, Mister."

Rynert licked lips which had abruptly gone dry. "You the law?"

The boy shook his head.

"Six years ago," he replied. "That day in the Central Valley. Wagon of German settlers, west of Sacramento."

Rynert's eyes widened. He looked hard and seemed to recognize something in the youth's face. He touched the brim of his hat, to give himself a moment to recover; but as he did, his fingers began to tremble. In that moment, his body seemed to contract itself, as though acknowledging that a greater force had entered the chamber. The other diners felt it too, and seemed to know that events would now be taking an entirely new trajectory.

"You?"

Rynert's voice sounded scratchy now, dry-throated, not at all like it had before, when he was taunting the helpless girl, surrounded as she had been by cowards.

No words escaped the boy, but his steady breathing answered the question. A grave silence took hold in the saloon hall, the silence of sadness and understanding, the lonely kind of silence that has no measure in time, the kind you might hear in a forest, or in a very deep cave that was far from any living thing.

"We nearly had you last year," the boy said. "Tracked you to the Two Bar Cross. Lost you in that dust storm."

Rynert's eyes flickered to the old tracker with a squirrel rifle who stood in the corner.

"Figured you'd come botherin' these Grangers, sooner or later," explained the blue-eyed boy.

Revenge is a large part of what makes us civilized. Before there were judges, and prisons, and sheriffs, and written codes of law, there was this one natural law: *Harm me and be harmed*. There is a price to pay. Monkeys and wolves and men all recognize the rule of retribution. It is justice, and symmetry, and (in its own harsh way) harmony; it is that glimmering – that my teeth or my sleeping throat or my innocent children will be at bloody risk – that makes each of us hesitate before doing all of what we sheerly want to do.

Revenge is a large part of what makes us civilized.

So it was in that saloon. All manner of nationalities filled the vacuum in those early days of the California territories – Swedes, Germans, Irishmen, Scots,

Mexicans, Comanche, French, Cossack -- each with their own conventions. Whether or not they recognized the boy, or personally knew of Rynert, or believed the one to be guilty and the other the avenger, they all recognized the play on stage.

Rynert drew first, then the redhead at his elbow.

The boy shot stepping forward. He slammed three quick rounds into Rynert's chest. A Colt appeared in his other hand and shot the redhead twice in the forehead.

A booming blast from his companion's squirrel gun sent the fourth gunman sailing through a window.

Smoke hovered, rising slowly over all that death, in the saloon.

The Granger girl broke into sobs.

The big man beside her moaned.

A chair squeaked on the wood planks of the floor.

"Mite slow with that left hand," commented the tracker.

A lingering shard of glass from the shattered window teetered in its caulking and fell, and broke, producing a tinkling sound, like a bell.

The boy grunted.

"Justice dealt by man," said one of the women, "comes with a price."

"It shorely does, ma'am," replied the youth.

He fed bullets in his pistol chamber until it was full again. He shucked it back into its holster.

"Two more to go. Then may be we can talk about justice."

AFTERWORD

1871
Sierra Madres, California territory
Range war between cattlemen and farmers

This work derives from my infatuation with Louis L'Amour. It is a remnant of a vast busted fiction project from my late twenties.

My students like this one because it is really short and they can pick out the story components we study (rising action, dialogue, conflict, anagnorisis, time frame, foreshadowing, falling action) fairly easily. It also has that immigration theme that becomes useful when we study The *Great Gatsby, The Godfather, Ragtime*, and other assimilation stories. I remind them of the German boy when we get to the Civil War lesson plans, since the community of German Americans was so crucial in that conflict.

The setting is northern California in the cowboy years, when a number of powerful historic and economic elements came together. This post-Civil War period is one of my favorite, very brief but very influential. The nation was sick of war, a modern world loomed just over the horizon, and a certain lawlessness set in during the all-at-once westward expansion. Every generation redefines what America is, they say, and that particular American generation's struggle for identity still echoes today.

CHARACTERS
The German Boy was only nine years old when his family's wagon train was captured. His grim quest to find the men responsible for the dark deed is completed in a saloon, six years down the road.

I had a darker version of Jack Kirby's *Rawhide Kid* in mind for the lead character in this story. His laconic trapper companion comes straight out of Louis L'Amour's *Sacketts* landscape. After this encounter, the Kid goes on to hunt down the last two members of the gang that ended his family's lives. Things get nasty, since one of them is now a respected lawman.

If the Granger girl were to figure into the next chapters, she would need a storyline and a quest of her own.

* * *

In the cycle of empire literature, most Westerns fall into the second station, "Rise of Empire," stories which detail the methods and challenges of dominating both nature and other cultures in order to build an empire. Almost all war stories are category three, High Empire, depicting the defending of the realm. All science fiction is category four, Collapse of Empire.

The Western hero's rival is the detective hero, namely Sherlock Holmes. This model rose at the same time as the cowboy, and has a very different response to the particular evils of the modern world – he sits in a comfortable chair and thinks about it. Where the cowboy hero wins by strength, fearlessness, and ordeals of self-denial, Sherlock wins by his smarts. Sherlock and all his descendant-heroes live in cities, where you cannot really tell who the enemy is.

Not only is his setting very different, so is Sherlock's mission. The detective's main goal is write a new theory of the truth, where all the false fronts are gone, revealing who is who. Bringing the bad guy to justice is an afterthought.

The Rawhide Kid crawls through a canyon in order to win a gunfight. Sherlock Holmes gathers information and then harvests it, weaving a new version of reality. One is savage and silent, the other is highly civilized and well-spoken. Two very distinct heroes for the modern age …

Love Triangle in the High Sierras

"There was a feel of things growing here,
of a rich, dark soil bursting with eagerness
to grow beneath my feet."

The First Fast Draw

Art by Boell Oynio
Color by Javelin Studio

"IT SEEMS SO PEACEFUL FROM UP here."

Dave Durrell, a young man who was not good with words, had rehearsed the comment. Now that he had said it, it sounded forced.

That was a dumb thing to say. She can see that for herself!

The horses grazed on the bluff as Angie and the young deputy sheriff, Durrell, looked over the valley. Cap Preshaw, her father's foreman, filled his canteen in the shade on the far side of the stream, pretending to pay no attention to the young couple.

"It's beautiful," she said.

They could see men moving already through the wheat rows far below. The soft noise of the horses' jaws munching grass resonated in the early morning air.

"Peaceful now. Range war soon enough," said Durrell. "I can feel it coming."

"It's not your fight," said Angie.

"Reckon it is. One way or th' other."

Stupid! Why did you bring that up? Durrell silently berated himself.

Dave Durrell was young, and clumsy with his emotions, but he had lived some of life. He had fought with Grant, at Pittsburgh Landing (or Shiloh, as the Rebels called it), and had seen at Hornet's Nest just how savage close combat can get. He had picked up an Enfield from a dead Reb and never gave ground after, and now it never left his side. Durrell was one of those competent, quiet young men whom the War had changed forever; they could not go back to what they had known, so they wandered the West, moving from job to job.

He had recently been hired by the town of Twin Lakes to slow the cattlemen and their simmering violence until the Federal Judge arrived. But now rumors of imported gunmen bounced around Little Squaw Valley on the western slope of the High Sierras, and last week two of the Swede's best cows had died in a barn fire of mysterious origin. Now men walked on the streets of the high-meadow town slowly, with their arms slightly away from their bodies. They waited for a man on the street to pass until he was clear.

* * *

Our history is the history of food.

Our history is the history of food.

Our leaders are always, and only, those with the ability to feed us. All their actions serve to preserve that supply: if they lose that ability, we kill them. The *muriophorio* merchant ships with their 500 tons of capacity crossed the Mediterranean, bringing Rome the enormous quantities of grain from Egypt, from Sicily, from northern Africa, grain needed to feed the empire's people. The Romans built a navy to guard the *muriophorio*, and sailed them with rigorous security procedures to protect the grain: with no intermediate stops, they could only be unloaded at the port of Ostia, or Pozzuoli, where cheering crowds welcomed the grain fleets. The wheat was then inspected and barged up the Tiber to the warehouses where the Emperor could distribute grain free to his grateful citizens. Then meat-eating invaders, Goths and Vandals and Franks, swarmed the collapsing Roman Empire; but the barbarians offered no system of food growing and distribution to replace the imperial system, and they fell, plunging Europe into a dark, chaotic era of famine and poverty.

And now America had discovered the explosive growing properties of California land. Grass for cattle and wheat for bread, the soils nurtured whatever man planted. And, as always, men gathered to clash over the harvest.

In the preceding decade, the ideal climate and fertile soils of the Sacramento Valley had produced far more wheat than the citizens of California could eat. The families who had travelled across the Atlantic from Sweden and Germany and Ireland now migrated to California, and were growing wheat and corn on a scale unknown since the inland empires of the ancient Maya. The rich soils of the open American prairies produced farms unlike any ever seen. Conditions in California did not favor cotton. A colony of growers tried sericulture, the farming of mulberry bushes and silk worms, but the climate was not quite right. With enough irrigation water, oranges and strawberries and lettuce would follow.

Citrus could only be grown in irrigated desert valleys or along hillsides where natural air drainage prevented frosts. Wheat, however, was different. No irrigation was needed, and the grain was hardy enough to be transported without damage. By 1850, over 18,000 farms were registered in Central Valley. A Canadian engineer named George Chaffey diverted water from the Colorado River into the Imperial Valley. Under-manned, the pioneer California farmers fiddled with procedures and adapted some of the European devices to suit their own needs. Under the stress of their struggle with nature they found new methods which worked on the limitless land.

But then they had to fight the cattlemen.

Europe craved beef as well as grain, and the cattlemen sold their beef at handsome markup to the hungry maw of the Eastern seaboard marketplaces. Cattle breeders had introduced pedigreed stock from Europe. Their herds needed huge expanses of grasslands, tracts of open prairie, and these men were not shy about claiming land, legally or otherwise.

The wheat caravan carrying Angie Cass's family's wheat to San Francisco would depart in two days. McGonigle and his bullies would try to stop it at Durango Pass. The cattlemen had to prevent that wheat from making it to market; the successful sale of all that fat golden high-meadow wheat would fill the Grangers Bank coffers, giving the farmers the means to dig in, even to expand their land holdings. That would not do; not for a cattleman like McGonigle, a man who was used to calling the shots.

* * *

But Dave Durrell did not have mountain passes or land rights on his mind this morning. Since he had first laid eyes on Angie Cass, he could think of nothing else.

He had never met anyone like her. Strong, independent, smart, she rode a horse as well as any man. If she lacked some of the shallow city graces of the girls he had known in St. Louis, well, she surely made up for it with her rich laughter. And on Sundays, the way she filled out that gingham dress … Well, any man would want a woman like that beside him.

"Listen, Angie. I … I, ah …"

What's wrong with me? Durrell cursed himself silently. *Why are my hands shaking?*

"My … my, uh …" His mouth could not seem to form the words.

Angie Cass glanced up. Barely sixteen, she had the knowing eyes of a woman.

"Look here, Miss Ange. I'm twenty-three years old. My father was an Irishman who drank too much and got hisself shot. I was fourteen. That's when I joined the 77th Ohio.

"Now, I got a sister in Olathe who means the world to me. I got thirteen hundred dollars, a Texas leather saddle, a shotgun and two rifles to my name. I can cook and I can stitch some. And I plan on staking out some o' that land up by Gustafson's place when things die down."

A breeze ruffled through the long grass, and through the leaves in the surrounding trees. Below, in the distance, they could see men moving through rows of wheat, harvesting the biggest crop in years. The horses glanced up and returned to their grazing. Dave Durrell's heart raced. Strong emotions coursed through him.

A man is a thinking being, a self-aware creature, with a brain that can cast numbers into the future, or calculate the construction of a steel bridge across a thousand-year-old gorge. But he is an animal, too, and deep springs of passion well up in him, and no man does himself good by ignoring those wild calls.

"So now I know," said Angie with a smile.

"So now you know," said Durrell. "But I do mean to ask you—"

The horses suddenly jerked and turned.

* * *

The sound of hooves rose on the trail behind them. They turned in their saddles and saw riders emerge from the tree-shrouded trail, two by two, until a dozen of them had appeared. The way the riders spread out carefully, blocking the pass, told all.

"Mornin', Miss Angie."

"What are you doing here?" Angie asked Dirk McGonigle.

"Enjoying the view," said McGonigle. "Same as you."

McGonigle did not mask his intent. He and the Bar B had the jump on them, on all of them, on the entire valley of slow-footed, slow-moving farmers. He would start here and press forward until they were shoved off the land like dominoes off a board. *Resolve is victory*, he liked to say, and he had made up his mind many months ago.

The Valley was about to discover his simple plan.

"Federal judge will be here Monday, Dirk," said Durrell, turning his horse to face the Bar B riders. "We can settle it then."

"I'll give him your regrets, Deputy," smirked the cattleman. A low laugh mixed with the other, pleasant sounds of that Sierra morning, swishing among the rustling leaves. A rope -- a California lariat, longer than the Texas ropes -- was tossed high into the air. It loped around a sturdy branch and held fast.

Dave Durell bitterly cursed himself for a fool.

I should have known McGonigle would try something --

"Go ahead, McGonigle," came a new voice, steely cold.

"Make your play."

Cap Preshaw had stepped from the dappled shade on the far side of the creek. He was a slim man, sinewy and tan in his blue Army shirt. The Henry .44 repeating rifle, which carried 15 rounds of long, deadly cartridges in its magazine, and which he held in his right hand, was aimed directly at Dirk McGonigle. Sunlight and shade alternated over the earthly form of Cap Preshaw as the breeze ruffled the tree leaves above him; sunlight glinted on the weapon's barrel.

"Now's as good a time as any," Cap said casually, although his tense stance and the stone-cold feature of his face were anything but casual.

In the long silence that followed, calculations were made. The odds had not changed, but the sequence had; McGonigle himself would be the first to die. Doubt had crept into the line of Bar B henchmen. The gunman Brodie leaned forward and spat. *Who would pay the gunmen if McGonigle was dead?* Odd things pop into a man's mind at times like this. One of the horses whinnied nervously.

"I seen hats like that in El Paso," said Preshaw to the stranger riding beside McGonigle. "You from El Paso?"

"Yup."

Doubt had crept into the line of Bar B henchmen.

"You Soderman? You the one who killed Sam Picco's son?"

"Reckon so," replied Soderman.

"Good," said Preshaw. "Then you can be second—"

Preshaw let go with the Henry and two violent booms smashed the quiet.

All hell broke loose.

Soderman fell, his half-drawn pistol firing harnlessly into the earth. The second shot split Raglin's skull near in two.

Cap Preshaw moved to his right, directly towards the main body of the Bar B crowd.

He's drawing fire away from us –

Dave Durrell pulled his rifle from its scabbard and fired and drove his horse forward and fired again. He needed badly to upset the Bar B gunmen, who were not expecting a fair fight; he could not let them remember their advantage. He spread fire along the line as he approached. He saw three of them fall and another three bolt for the trees.

Nevada Ed clutched his throat and fell, gurgling blood.

Brodie slid backwards off his saddle, bucked or shot.

Two more booming rounds from Cap and John Ginty grunted and died, shot twice in the side. Cap advanced openly, like a berserker, seeking only to inflict harm.

He's doing it for her, realized Durrell. *He is drawing all the fire to himself --*

Dave Durrell let out a scream like the rebel yells he had heard at the Hornet's Nest, when Wallace had weakened and the day seemed lost. It was a feral sound, half-mad and half-banshee, and it shook the Bar B. Two more fell from their saddles. Durrell knew they would not be getting back up; the Enfield fired .557 shells, and few men survived being struck by a bullet as long as that.

Out of the corner of his eye he was aware that Angie had whipped her hunting rifle from scabbard and was firing with care and consistency.

Ugh --

Durrell felt a sting in his shoulder and, in a rush, he was spun from the saddle. From the ground, as if in a dream, the deputy saw Preshaw crouched low and firing with deadly accuracy even as he crossed the stream.

McGonigle aimed his long-barreled pistol and hit Cap.

Angie took aim, paused to make sure, and buried three quick rounds in McGonigle's chest.

Terribly wounded, Cap kept advancing. Now he tossed the Henry aside and now he fired his pistol, fanning the hammer to spray as much lead as he still could. Cap had downed four Bar B men before he had crossed the creek.

God in heaven, thought Durrell, almost idly, as if in a dream. *No man anywhere can shoot like that --*

Two of the riders' horses bolted. From his knees, Durrell picked off one and then the burning in his shoulder racked his body and brain like lighting exploding. He blacked out for an instant.

He shook his head clear. He saw that McGonigle's henchmen were in retreat. All their taste for bullying had fled as soon as death – real, bullet-driven, bloody death and final agony -- had reared its head.

"CAPPY!"

Angie's cry was a wild sound, something elemental, and it carried such a depth of feeling that it raised the hair on the young sheriff's forearms.

She threw herself off the saddle into the stream where Preshaw had fallen with a recklessness Durrell had seen once before, at Seven Timbers, when the Confederate officer, Forrest, took a musket round in his hip and still managed to ride.

Dave Durrell watched Angie disappear beneath the water's surface and then reappear, clutching Cap's body.

Or is he still -- ?

Suddenly Ginty rose from the ground and trained his gun on the two figures in the stream. Durrell yanked his left-hand pistol from its holster and shot him twice, three times; the last Bar B gun fell silent.

Angie pulled Cap to the grassy riverbank.

She murmured into his ear.

Preshaw coughed up water. Without his hat, Cap didn't look much older than the girl.

Cap Preshaw's eyes opened. He looked up the girl holding him so tightly and smiled at her. It was a most familiar smile, the kind you give to someone whom you know very, very well.

"Don't you ever do that again," she told him. She kissed him.

Ah, thought Dave Durrell, as he struggled to his feet, holding his shoulder to staunch the blood.

I didn't understand …

Ahh, thought Dave Durrell … *I didn't understand.*

AFTERWORD

Love Triangle in the High Sierras
1871, Sierra Madres, California territory
Range war between cattlemen and farmers

My imitation of Louis L'Amour, part II. I once had a larger plot going with these three characters but, as you can see, I never really broke into new ground.

The idea behind this story is how teen-aged boys are consumed with their own passions, to the exclusion of all else. Beyond that, I don't think there is much original that I offer readers in this story.

The setting is northern California in the cowboy years, when a number of powerful historic and economic elements came together. This post-Civil War period is one of my favorite, very brief but very influential. The nation was sick of war, a modern world loomed just over the horizon, and a certain lawlessness set in during the all-at-once westward expansion. Every generation redefines what America is, they say, and that particular American generation's struggle for identity still echoes today.

CHARACTERS
Dave Durrell is like my older cadets – game but not entirely clued in. A little self-absorbed. He is smart and brave, but not nearly enough so to survive that trap alone.

As for the artwork, Boell Oyino can really draw!! While many illustrators are dazzled by the charms of digital painting (and with good reason), accomplished draftsmanship always delivers. Boell makes it look easy.

* * *

If you like heroes, you need to read Jane Tompkins' *West of Everything*. I recently interviewed her and wrote a journal article (*www.empirestudies.com*) that gives an introduction to her excellent ideas.

The Western is such a big deal in the family of narratives because it sets the model for the American hero that we see today. Compare the protagonists of most contemporary films and you come up with the same set of attributes – the hero is stoic, resilient, language-averse, glory-averse, good at fighting of all kinds, attractive to women, and someone who brings his own moral authority with him. This is the cowboy hero, searching for his identity and seeking justice in hostile landscapes. In Jane Tompkins' words:

> The hero, provoked by insults, first verbal, then physical, resists the urge to retaliate, proving his moral superiority to those who taunt him ... The villains, whoever they may be, finally commit an act so atrocious that the hero must retaliate in kind.

The cowboy is a special sort of American myth that each generation tells in its own way. It has an extended set of heroic symbols, structures and conventions, in which we take delight, today more than ever.

Frederic Remington's "Shotgun Hospitality (1908) Wikimedia Commons

The first rule of Western heroes is that they only strike back after having been wronged. The second rule is that they hate talking. The third rule is that they love the landscape so much that they *become* the landscape.

All good cowboys reject talking – it is depicted as a sort of trick, a device to fool an honest man. "The Western's attack on language is wholesale and unrelenting," Jane Tompkins writes. "Language constitutes and inferior kind of reality, and the farther one stays away from it the better." What language we do find in cowboy stories Tompkins describes as "abstract." I take this to mean that the short and mysterious sentences which the heroes give out do not connect to what is actually happening in the story, but veer off into a higher dimension, making some other kind of sense.

Silent and stoic, the lands of the American West act as a sort of cure or offset to the evils of words. "The interaction between hero and landscape lies at the genre's center," Tomkins writes. "In the end, the land is everything to the hero; it is both the destination and the way." Here she clarifies this connection between hero and landscape:

> And so men imitate the land in Westerns; they try to look as much like nature as possible … The qualities needed to survive on the land are the qualities the land itself possesses – bleakness, mercilessness. And they are regarded not only as necessary to s urvival but as the acme of moral perfection.

If you're like me, you'll think of this the next time you watch *The Revenant*.

You should read *Kilkenny* or *The Sackett Brand* or *Trail to Seven Pines* or almost anything else by Louis L'Amour. His work has something that mine does not have – that quality of lighting a fire in his readers, making us *need* to find out what happens next.

CALIFORNIA

Ulysses S. Grant in China

The Prince saluted General Grant in Tartar fashion, looking at him for a moment with an earnest, curious gaze, like one who had formed an ideal of some kind and was anxious to see how far his ideal had been realized.

-- J.F. Packard, *Grant's Tour Around the World*

PART I. A TRIO BECOMES A QUARTET

"You must *flower* when you come in on that stanza, Ning Po," said the Instructor.

"I cannot flower, Madame," replied Ning Po.

The music continued. It was a simple melody, made somewhat more challenging by the counter-melody which the Instructor herself was playing.

"The piece is entirely constructed around that moment," said the Instructor to Ning Po.

"I can flower," offered Soo Ching, Ning Po's younger brother.

"I know you can, Soo Ching. Just try and keep the tempo, will you?"

The grand and unique recital chamber in the Chinese house was divided between a wooden-floored music room on the left and a rock garden with small flowering trees and boulders and a sandstone wall, on the right. The back wall of the recital room was dominated by a rectangular window with a spectacular view of Tientsin's main square.

The dimensions of the room were so large as to be American. An open garden was rare in the city, especially one overlooking the center of Tientsin. It was a most cosmopolitan city, in the year 1879, one which harbored little compounds of Europe -- French, Russian, Italian, English and German legations living in small cul-de-sacs reminiscent of their home cultures. Lively commerce filled its streets, barely masking currents of unrest.

The room featured a discreet gallery of paintings on its ivory walls, a showcase in a private house with a public purpose. The acoustics were as remarkable as the view.

"We are *terrible,*" commented Pao Shan.

"Hush, Pao Shan," said the Instructor.

"She's right," said Soo Ching.

"When Uriah Ess Grant hears how bad we are, he will rise from his chair and go back to America," said Pao Shan.

"He survived the Battle of Shiloh," replied the Instructor. "I think he will find a way to survive our concert."

The City of Tientsin prepared for the arrival of the upcoming visit of the brave American General. Even the peasants had heard (if not read) of his battle victories, and his service in the Mexican wars, and his ascendance to the Presidency, his perseverance at Vicksburg, and in particular his gallantry in victory -- how the gracious Grant tipped his hat to Robert E. Lee on the front porch, and how he held back from punishing the defeated armies of the South. He detested war even as he claimed superiority. He was one of the most celebrated men alive. Men, women and children gathered in the tens of thousands to see him pass by on a train, and to sing tributes. Cannons and speeches, music recitals and long dinners greeted him in London and Venice and Calcutta … and now Tientsin.

Viceroy Li Hong Zhang, himself a most remarkable leader, would soon welcome him.

"Stop!" called the Instructor.

The trio of young musicians came to a ragged halt.

She cocked her ear. "Can you hear?"

They all strained to listen. Through the window, they could hear music wafting … it was a *chaunqi,* one of the five melodies of traditional Sichuan Opera. While the collective sound of many instruments was impressive, the melody was being played slowly and without verve.

"That," said the Instructor, "is our Imperial Orchestra. They are practicing the opera piece they will play for the Great Warrior -- "

"Ugh!" said Soo Ching. "The American President will hate it. I hate it."

"We follow them," said the Instructor. "The audience will be happy to hear our simple folk song. If only Ning Po can play with some kind of verve …"

"All the Internationals are playing in the concert," said Pao Shan. "I hear them practicing at night. The Scots will win. Everyone loves those bagpipes."

"We will get last place," said Ning Po.

"The Spanish drums are my favorite," said Soo Ching.

"Why are we speaking English?" asked Pao Shan.

"It is a global age, Pao Shan," said the Instructor.

"*Da shui zhong ne long wang mian,*" replied Pao Shan. "We are Chinese!"

"*Lao ji fu li, zhi zai qian li,*" added Ning Po.

"None the less." The Instructor ignored Ning Po's unfortunate choice of words. "English is the language the rest of the world speaks."

The Instructor picked up a flute.

"Now. The Viceroy has asked me to compose a brief refrain celebrating the new China. A piece of music which all the legations might share.

"Here it is. See what you think."

She played a 12-bar passage of her own composition on the flute.

"Let's try it," she said.

The trio of teens picked up their instruments and gave the simple melody a try. Soo Ching liked it.

"Again. One, two three ...

"Awful!" she laughed after three more tries. "It must be the composer!"

"Once more!" called Soo Ching.

"My fingers ache," said Ning Po.

"You've done a good work morning's work," said the Instructor. "God willing, we will be ready for Ulysses S. Grant. Take a ten-minute break."

Suddenly the sharp crack of rifle fire echoed in the music room.

"What is THAT?" cried Soo Ching.

The trio dropped their instruments and ran to the windows to see what caused the noise.

"Is it the rebels?" asked Pao Shan. "They say there was an attack on a payroll wagon in Beijing last week..."

"The *jiangxi* are firing their rifles for General Grant," guessed the Instructor.

"What idiots," concluded Soo Ching. "It is only the American advance party arriving ..."

"How do you know that?" asked Pao Shan

"Our father is helping plan the visit," replied Soo Ching. "He has associates who are visiting soon. He was talking about it at breakfast."

More rifle shots sounded. Next came the boom of a cannon, followed by the distant sound of a cheering crowd.

Mother swept through the double doors to see what the commotion could be.

A petite woman, she wore a formal gown with a high collar and wooden slippers that clattered slightly on the polished floor.

Her attendant, Pi-Chi (who was Pao Shan's mother) came with her, standing between the teenagers and Mother.

Mother went directly to the window, shading her face with one hand. Soo Ching and Ning Po looked at her.

"Mother!" said Soo Ching. "What happened to your f--"

"A hundred thousand people are gathered on the riverbanks," announced Pi-Chi.

"Just to get a glimpse of his boat. They sang him songs. All the way from Yongle to Wuking."

"Can you imagine?" said the Instructor.

"Where did they get all those rifles …?" asked Soo Ching.

"I don't know what all the fuss is about anyway," said Pao Shan.

"General Grant is a great man," answered the Instructor. "He led his people to freedom."

"I thought Lincoln did that," said Ning Po.

"Well, he did, but Grant helped. Do you know the re-- "

They were interrupted by a loud and violent knock on the front door. The bells hung at the entrance rang in a panic. They heard steps, followed by a commotion among the staff. They heard one of the staff open the front door. A conversation ensued.

A voice called for Madame Xi Ping (which was Mother's name).

Mother and Pi Chi rushed out of the music room to see what the matter might be.

The trio and the Instructor listened to the ensuing discussion. Madame Xi Ping's voice was so soft that everyone had to lean into the doorway to hear her. The matter apparently concluded. The front door slammed shut. The bells rang again.

The door to the music recital room opened.

An American youth entered the recital room.

He was taller than the Chinese teens, dressed in a military uniform of Union blue with brass buttons, a neckerchief and white shirt.

He was carrying a case.

He bowed.

The Instructor bowed.

The boy handed the Instructor a letter.

She opened the letter and read it aloud.

"It says that this is an American boy who is a member of General Grant's entourage."

There was a slight *gasp* at this news.

"Viceroy Li-Hong Zhang recommends that he join our group," the Instructor continued, "and that he participate in our musical tribute."

She looked up. "How fitting! And what is your name, *laowai*?"

"Joseph," he answered. "Joseph Seward."

He shook hands vigorously with the Instructor, who tried to bow and shake hands at once.

"Joseph Seward, you are most welcome."

"This is Pao Shan. Flute.

"This is Soo Ching. Drums.

"This is Ning Po. Violin."

The Instructor pulled up a fourth chair for Joseph to sit in.

"What instrument do you play?"

"I can play this." He removed a banjo from the case he was carrying. "And this." He took a harmonica from his shirt pocket.

"How extraordinary! What is it?"

Instead of answering, Joseph placed his knee on the chair and began playing. The banjo made an explosion of sound in the recital room. The rude sound seemed to bang off the walls and start all over again. He strummed faster, like a train. The sound startled the group, none of whom had heard such a powerful sound. He alternated between chords and picking the strings individually; the richness and strangeness were overwhelming.

"What was THAT?" demanded Soo Ching, delighted.

"How do you do that?" asked Pao Shan.

Joseph picked up the harmonica and played a rollicking tune. He kept time by stamping his feet. He popped his cheeks to punctuate the rhythm.

"What is that?" asked Soo Ching.

"A harmonica."

"A what?" asked Pao Shan.

"A harmonica."

"Because it only plays harmony?" asked Ning Po.

"Hah!" The young American friend of Grant, Joseph, played a deliberately dissonant version of "Oh!, Susanna." He then corrected the melody, then played faster, banging the harmonica against his free hand and alternately making popping sounds on his cheeks.

Ning Po put her hands over her ears.

"Can you teach me to do that?" asked Pao Shan.

Then they picked up their own instruments and joined in, even the Instructor, playing a cacophonic Mandarin version of "Oh!, Susanna" with Pao Shan trying to plunk the banjo as if it were a mandolin.

The Instructor, a most gifted musician, played a counter-melody. Joseph laughed.

He grabbed a chair and beat a rugged fast rhythm.

Soo Ching took the harmonica the instant Joseph put it down and immediately tried to isolate single notes that somehow fit the bouncing tune.

Ning Po rose from her seat and played standing up as the five musicians somehow managed to produce a raucous mix of American folk music and Chinese folk music.

Now they all stood and played their instruments, and then marched around the room. The Instructor interrupted to change the tune, bringing temporary chaos, but, after a pause to find the right key, the others joined in.

They played with abandon, even when Mother and her attendant came in to see what the ruckus was. Joseph's harmonica found the chords beneath the melody and played only those. Ning Po did the same. Soo Ching laughed.

The infectious music overflowed with all the feeling that was previously absent.

The Instructor drew a close to the recital.

"So now we are a quartet!"

PART II. ARCHERY IN THE MUSIC ROOM

A week later, the recital room echoed with sounds. Bagpipes being played in the Square mixed with Soo Ching's music. The youth was practicing the banjo, which fascinated him, as the others practiced archery in the rock garden.

"No!" insisted Joseph, standing with Ning Po in the garden. "*Snap it!*"

Ning Po pulled the bowstring back along her cheek.

"Further…" said Joseph.

She drew it taut.

"Snap it like you mean it!"

Ning Po let loose. The arrow plunked against the target and fell away.

"God Almighty, what are you so scared of?" Joseph notched another arrow for her.

"Yelling at me does not help," sulked Ning Po.

"Something better help." Joseph smiled. "Here … now stretch that back …"

"That's too far! It'll snap!"

"No, it won't …more … Now! Let 'er loose!"

"*Kong xue lai feng wei bi wu yin!*" protested Ning Po.

This time the arrow produced a resonant "thunk!" and thrust deep into the target.

"There! Finally!" said Joseph." Unless you hear that 'thunk', it's like you haven't shot at all."

"What is the Great Warrior like?" asked Pao Shan.

"Quiet. Smart. Very observant. He will ask you about something you said a week earlier."

"Were you in the Battle of Gettysburg?" asked Soo Ching

"Naw. I was three years old when it ended."

"Have you ever been in a battle? I mean, shooting someone?" asked Pao Shan.

"I was in an Indian skirmish once. What is Li Hong Zhang like?" asked Joseph.

There was a pause before the answer came.

"He is no doubt a great man," said Pao Shan. "A *controversial* man."

"That's not what my father says," said Ning Po.

"Yes, well your father should know -- " said Pao Shan

"Watch yourself -- " warned Ning Po.

"Why? Because you're rich?" demanded Pao Shan.

Ning Po dropped her bow. "No! Because my family has its problems. I know that! You don't have to *remind me* -- "

The Instructor entered and tapped her baton.

She called the class to order.

"All right! Only two more days before the concert. Let's start with that new passage that Joseph had for us."

The quartet sat down in their chairs and readied their instruments.

"Soo Ching, never play the banjo again," requested the Instructor. "That's an awful sound, my goodness."

Suddenly Father entered the recital room with two associates, a Cantonese man wearing black silk pants and tunic and a Cantonese youth who accompanied him.

The Quartet began to play.

It was a new tune, an American folk song which they had adapted to Chinese instrumentation.

Father looked on with pride as the Quartet played. He waved his hand as if he were holding a baton.

His associates measured the window, first on the outside, recording its dimensions, and then looking out of the window itself and down onto the Square with a scope, as if to measure distances. They pointed to the small balcony, clearly wondering if they could climb out and all fit onto it.

Mother swept into the room in a rush of silk and shouts. Something was wrong.

She spoke angrily and ordered the men out of her home. She repeated her order in several dialects.

"Get away from that window, sir!"

Father was furious at the interruption. "Get back to your chamber, woman!" Things were going very wrong, now.

Father cursed bitterly.

He moved menacingly towards his wife.

"No!" cried Ning Po.

Pi Chi moved between them. "How dare you -- "

"Hey!" cried Soo Ching. "Don't -- "

"Shut up," the Cantonese man warned Soo Ching darkly.

Mother renewed her protests.

Then Father tossed Pi Chi aside and struck Mother a wicked blow. That was the moment when everything changed. It was not a reserved blow, or a cautioning blow to prevent further discussion, but a savage strike across the mouth, one meant to inflict real harm. The petite Madame was flung reeling to the floor. Blood flew.

"*Father!*" Soo Ching rushed to stop him from delivering a second blow --

The Instructor moved to protect Madame Xi Ping as well.

The Cantonese man grabbed Soo Ching by the collar.

"I told you to shut your mouth -- " Father added a vile oath that had not been heard in those chambers before.

Father grabbed Mother by her elegant hair and slammed her face on the floor in an act that was all the more shocking because it had a familiar aspect to it, as though these two actors had played the scene more than once: *This had happened before.*

An arrow struck Father in the shoulder.

Time stood still in the pretty room.

Innocent sounds from the streets below floated in.

Father looked in disbelief at the brightly colored feathers on the shaft embedded in his shoulder. A red stain began to form on his clothing.

"Take your hands off her," said Ning Po calmly.

A second arrow struck his other shoulder. He winced in pain and surprise.

"Right now."

Ning Po notched a third arrow and aimed it at her father's head.

A weak groan escaped Mother, face-down on the elegant floor.

Ning Po stretched her bow back.

For a moment, Father did not know what to do.

Then a smile slowly took shape on his face: he had decided Ning Po would not, could not, shoot him again. His hand re-gripped Mother's hair --

Then several things happened at once:

First, the Cantonese man lunged to stop Ning Po –

Second, Ning Po let loose. The arrow struck Father in side of his neck. He let the Mother go and stood, stumbling --

Third, an arrow struck the Cantonese man in the ribs, sending him falling against the wall. A second shaft followed, pinning his sleeve with a satisfying, thick sound.

Joseph stepped forward, his bow already notched with a new arrow.

"What kind of man are you?" he rasped to the prone Father.

He swiveled and let loose a third arrow, which struck the Cantonese henchman straight in the throat, killing him.

They heard the sounds of breaking glass and chimes and shouts and furious scuffling on the stairs.

"The caves," said the Instructor to the children as she bolted the doors.

"Pao Shan – *the caves --* "

She and Pi Chi carried the Mother to a doorway hidden along the near wall. "We've got to hide her. We will meet you there."

"Daughter! Son!" cried Madame Xi Ping.

The teens rushed away. The Cantonese youth tried to stop them.

Joseph struck him hard across the head.

"Take him with us," said Ning Po.

When the doors finally buckled and the rebels rushed into the recital room, they were gone.

The framed paintings in the gallery looked down.

PART III. THE BATTLE OF THE CAVES OF TAKO WEI

Later, as day fell into night, five figures entered the forest glade.

Sparkling light from the city painted a faint glow in the moraine hills above Tientsin.

Trees and boulders created odd cavernous shapes in the foliage around the glade. Grass grew on the ledge above and in the tree-limned glen.

If you did not know of the cave entrance, you would never have seen it. The seam of the opening was parallel to the grain of jagged rocks jutting out, so that you had to be standing directly in front of it to see it.

Five figures groped in the semi-darkness as their eyes adjusted to the darkness. Ning Po went straight to the tunnel entrance that led to the cave and beckoned the others.

The interior of the tunnel was black and close, humid, low-ceilinged. Sounds hung in the still air.

"I think I've found the torches,"

whispered Pao Shan. "I knew they were here somewhere."

"Where are you?" asked Ning Po.

"Why are you whispering?" asked Soo Ching.

"Because they are looking for us," replied Pao Shan.

"Who is?"

"The police, for one," said Joseph.

"The rebels are looking for us, too," said Pao Shan, "since you had the bright idea of bringing him along." She nodded towards the Cantonese boy whom they had taken prisoner. "We should drop him off the cliff so they will stop hunting us."

"They won't stop," said Joseph. "We know their plan."

"What is their plan?" asked Soo Ching, surprised that they held this information.

"Why do you think they were measuring that window?" asked Joseph

"*Sssshhh!*" hissed Pao Shan. "I heard something."

This warning was followed by a long silence. Each listened carefully, but only the implacable sounds of the night could be heard.

Pao Shan struck a match.

The ragged group was illuminated: tired and dirty and ragged from their flight out of the city into the hills, they clustered in the mouth of the cave.

The light flickered and went out. Darkness returned.

"*Bun tyen-shung duh ee-dway-ro ...*" cursed Pao Shan bitterly.

"This is like a bad dream -- " groaned Soo Ching.

The torch was re-lit. Pao Shan shook her fingers, which had been singed by the flame.

Joseph dragged the prisoner deeper into the caves, following Pao Shan and her torch. Soo Ching found a second torch and lit it. Ning Po lagged behind as they clambered deeper into the cave.

"*Bun tyen-shung duh ee-dway-ro ...*" repeated Pao Shan.

"Speak English," said Ning Po weakly. "Joseph doesn't kn -- "

"I see the barrels!" said Pao Shan.

"I can't believe you shot Father -- " whined Soo Ching to his sister.

"I should have killed him," said Ning Po. "He hit Mother."

"It's not the first time," said Soo Ching.

"No, but it's the last."

Ning Po faltered.

"I can't believe you shot Father -- " whined Soo Ching to his sister. "I should have killed him," said Ning Po.

She slumped against the cave wall.

Joseph caught her and tenderly placed her on the ground. He made a pillow for her head. The prisoner slipped to the cave floor.

"Her face is like a ghost," remarked Soo Ching.

"What is wrong with her?" asked Pao Shan.

"She needs more opium," said the prisoner, who up to that point had shown neither human consciousness nor the capacity to speak English.

"What?" demanded Soo Ching.

"Why did you say that?" asked Joseph.

"*Take that back!*" said Pao Shan.

"I've seen it before," replied the prisoner firmly. "She's addicted. If she doesn't get more soon, she'll start shaking … real bad."

"She doesn't need *opium,*" insisted Soo Ching.

"Yes. I do," said Ning Po weakly.

She sat up, rallying.

"I can chew bark. That makes it go away for a while."

Each of the trio absorbed this cold fact in his or her own way as Ning Po searched the cave floor for bark. Joseph joined in the search.

"The barrels have water," offered Pao Shan. "Will that help?"

A light appeared in the grass above the cave, but they did not see it. A pair of heavily armed rebels was searching for the band of teens. They moved stealthily across the grass and into the forest.

"Look, our first problem is surviving the night," said Joseph.

"Our second problem is what happens in the morning."

"What do we do with him?" asked Pao Shan.

"We use him as a hostage if the rebels find us -- "

"It's not the rebels you should worry about," said the prisoner.

"What does that mean?" asked Joseph sharply.

The prisoner looked away and did not answer.

"What is going on?" Joseph demanded.

"A whole *lot* is going on," replied Pao Shan. "We are freezing to death. We have no food. We shot an Officer of the Prefecture -- "

"We had to!" protested Ning Po. "He was going to kill Mother --"

"That's not how he will tell it," said Pao Shan. "We are just a bunch of kids. Who do you think the Viceroy will believe?"

"They will believe Mother," answered Ning Po. "And the Instructor -- "

"Here it is!" announced Pao Shan.

They had come upon a cache of barrels and chests stacked along a nook in the cave walls. The light of the torches revealed trunks of weapons and clothing, blankets, provisions and equipment. One of the barrels held water. Pao Shan ladled water for Ning Po to drink.

"What is this place?" asked Joseph.

"Taku Wei!" said Pao Shan. "The Fortress of Tientsin used to be up here. We climbed up here all the time when we were kids."

"The Yongle Emperor fought in these hills. With his nephew," said the rebel boy. "One of their battles was near here."

"There are weapons -- " said Pao Shan.

"Look!"

Pao Shan held her torch with one hand and tipped one of the chests. She showed them bows and arrows, pistols and daggers. One spear.

Soo Ching found a box of pistols and wondered aloud if they were loaded.

They did not see it, but at that moment a lantern light appeared in the glen behind them, just outside the cave. A trio of heavily armed Imperial guards searched for the band of teens. They moved stealthily across the grass. Seeing nothing, they moved on.

Soo Ching donned a chain-metal coat, with big shoulders and padded sleeves. Joseph found a long-handled sword and Ning Po found a deeply-curved bow and then a sheath of arrows. A musty banner was draped across a row of shields.

"*Nenk gau yant fant ca,*" said the rebel boy. "*Mog gau yant da zay.*"

"What is that?" demanded Soo Ching. "Mandarin?"

"You look like idiots!" criticized the prisoner.

"First you practice songs to welcome the foreigners," he continued, "so they will be comfortable while they loot China. Now you mock the warriors of the past. That's *perfect*."

"They're not looting China -- " commented Pao Shan, as she held a shield to the light, so she could see its decorations.

"You don't know China," declared the prisoner.

"Oh, I know China -- " said Pao Shan.

"What do you mean, *laowai*?" asked Ning Po.

"You live in some fantasy world," stated the prisoner. "That palace you live in is not the real China."

"That's true," admitted Pao Shan.

"Real Chinese are in the fields. Working on the rivers, setting traps in the forest. Not being served on silver. Conversing in English."

"You don't know China," declared the prisoner. "Oh, I know China -- " said Pao Shan.

"*How bat fah shishume!*" spat Soo Ching.

"You can deny it all you want. China is being stripped." The rebel boy glared at his captors defiantly. "People like you and your father just usher the bandits in and out. And take their fees."

"What does that even mean?" asked Soo Ching.

"Where do you think we get our guns? How do you think your father affords your beautiful house overlooking Tienjin Square?"

"Father is an importer -- "

"He imports *guns*. And we pay him in *opium*," said the rebel.

"Take that back -- " said Soo Ching,

"Everything you think is important is meaningless," said the rebel, as if it were a reply.

Lantern lights appeared outside the cave, both above the incautious youth, in the grass on the cave's roof, and behind them, in the glen. Both the rebel patrol and the Imperial Guard had heard the voices. They had been discovered.

From above, heavily armed Imperial guards found a back entrance and began climbing down into the cave tunnel.

"Who are you?" demanded Ning Po. "Why were you in my house?"

"My name is Lu'k Kun."

"Are you English?" asked Pao Shan. "Why is your English so good?"

"My mother was Belgian. She was a school teacher."

"That name doesn't sound Belgian."

"It's not!"

Rebels discovered the cave mouth and argued as they prepared to come inside.

"I am a schoolteacher's son," said L'uk Kun. "My parents were murdered by the Guard. My sister died trying to protect them.

"I have nothing left to live for. But I will make my life count for something -- unlike you f-- "

"He is a member of the Boxer conspiracy," Joseph explained.

Now the Imperial Guards outside the cave could clearly hear the teens. They crept stealthily through the umbrage towards them.

From the opposite direction, the rebels were moving through the tunnel towards the unsuspecting five.

"How do you know that?" Ning Po asked Joseph.

"Tell me, Boxer – why that house?" Joseph asked L'uk Kun. "Why the interest in the window? Go ahead, tell them -- "

Feeling he had said too much, Lu'k Kun turned away.

"You were spying on that house because it had a view of the stands," Joseph explained.

"They mean to assassinate General Grant."

For a suspended moment, everyone was still. Lu'k Kun hid his face so the others could not see that it was true.

Then several important things happened at once:

The Imperial Guards rushed at them from the left.

The rebels rushed in from the right, yelling about worker's rights.

Soo Ching's pistol went off with a deafening "*boom!*"

The torches were dropped and the caves returned to darkness.

Pao Shan fell over a pile of metal armor with a great clatter.

In the next moment, the teens rushed as a group, scrambling, for the cave entrance.

"They mean to assassinate General Grant!" cried Ning Po.

They somehow emerged into the moonlight in the glade. Confusion reigned as three parties – rebels, teens and Imperial Guards – clanged and shouted and clashed, chasing around the little glen. The torches went out and progressions of escape and capture were played out in darkness. All manner of grunts and groans and shouted exclamations (in English, Mandarin and Cantonese) filled the glade. A shield clanged against something metal.

A horseman carrying a lantern emerged from the trees at the center of the grove.

For a long moment, the horseman dominated the scene without speaking. He raised a lantern; the light helped the commotion to quiet down. All parties stopped and looked: the rider was dramatically framed by the trees and limned in the light from torches carried by riders who now emerged from the forest behind him.

It was a large contingent.

Now they spread out, surrounding the grove.

"My name is Ulysses S. Grant," said the figure holding the lantern.

"Ah. There you are, Joseph." Grant's deep voice seemed to echo. The beard, the high collar, the profile limned in lantern-light, the glint of the hero's eye – it all had the power of a dramatic painting.

Soo Ching whimpered in disbelief.

"I am glad to see you are all well," he declared.

Grant's horse snickered and shook his head, tired of standing still.

"Why don't you and your friends come back to the Palace with us," said Ulysses S. Grant to Joseph, who carried Ning Po in his arms.

"We have been looking for you high and low. What will your father think?

PART IV. THE NIGHT BEFORE THE CONCERT

In a plain room with a wooden table and a grouping of chairs, Li-Hong Zhang and General Ulysses S. Grant held a private session with the teen quartet and their Instructor.

Guards lined the walls.

"These are most perilous times," said Viceroy Li Hong Zhang.

"We first heard of the Cantonese rebels during the winter. They have been planning to get at General Grant during his visit to Tientsin."

"Why?" asked the Instructor.

"In their minds," said the Viceroy, "General Grant represents the international powers who seek to corrupt China. Foreign invaders."

"I've been called worse," commented Grant. "By Democrats."

Li-Hong Zhang turned to Ning Po and Soo Ching. "We knew they were in contact with your father.

"Once the location of the Loochoo Court and the International concert were announced, we knew that they would seek to use your house. The location is perfect for their use.

"That is why we placed Joseph in your household," explained General Grant.

"Joseph is a spy?" asked Ning Po.

"He is an American soldier," said General Grant.

"He was to report back to us on activities in your household. I regret that we were too slow to protect you from the rebels."

"You were most brave in your actions," said Viceroy Li Hong Zhang. "We are grateful."

"Is my father a rebel?" asked Ning Po.

"No," answered the Viceroy. "He is a merchant who deals in guns."

"A gun smuggler?"

"I'm afraid so."

"And drugs as well?" asked Ning Po.

A long silence followed this question. No one felt inclined to answer it.

"Is he still alive?" asked Ning Po.

"He was last seen in Zhangzhou," replied the Viceroy. "He is now an enemy of the state. The rebel you killed," he said to Joseph, "was named Sho Tai. It was his plan."

"And L'uk Kun?" asked Pao Shan.

"He escaped at the caves," answered the Viceroy. "We think he will be hiding in the crowd, looking for a way to get to the General."

"To *shoot* him?" asked Pao Shan.

"Yes."

"Then you must call off the concert," concluded Pao Shan. "Call off the Loochoo Court."

"Half the male population of my own nation tried their best to kill me for three years," stated Grant. "I think I can hold up."

"Lu'k Kun is an experienced assassin," said Li-Hong Zhang.

"He's our age," Pao Shan disagreed. "He is just like us."

"Last month he garroted a French merchant on the Silk Road," the Viceroy informed them.

"We are the only ones who can recognize him," said the Instructor.

"We do not wish to place you in any more risk," said the Viceroy.

"Can you place guards around us as we play …?" asked the Instructor.

The Viceroy nodded, almost reluctantly.

"Then I am willing."

She turned to the Quartet.

"What do you think?"

Each of the players in turn nodded. In Pao Shan's case, it was a slow nod …

* * *

In his chambers, Viceroy Li-Hong Zhang was slightly more open with his opinions. He spoke to his aide, Cho.

"Do we have 300 ducats we can use to hire the Russian engineer? He helped build the Suez Canal, or so he says.

"We will need a canal or two before long, eh, Cho?

"We must interview him and see what he knows. Not all engineers can design. Some engineers repair doorknobs. A lengthy interview can save all sides the embarrassment, if it is discovered that the hired party has no capacity to do the job for which he was hired.

"Are you even listening?"

"Yes," replied Cho. "But not to you, to the music outside … "

The Viceroy cocked his head.

"Is that the China theme I commissioned? It sounds good."

"The Krupps have asked again for an appointment," said Cho. "They insist on bidding for the 10th Infantry armaments.'

"Huh," said Li Hong Zhang. "They can smell war coming. And war is the best business of all.

"Schedule them for next Wednesday. First thing in the morning. I cannot deal with Germans in the afternoon."

Li-Hong Zhang tapped his two front teeth with his forefinger, as he did when lost in his thoughts.

"Is everything set for tomorrow?"

"As much as it can be," answered Cho. "We have gone over and over every contingency."

"We have people in every legation?"

"Yes."

"General Grant has his heavy vest?"

"And three men to surround him."

"Let's make it four."

"The attack is expected at two o'clock?"

"Yes. The messages we intercepted were clear on that point."

"And the rebels are still under our observation?

"All but the boy. Lu'k Kun."

"His whereabouts?"

"Unknown."

"What else is unknown?" wondered Li-Hong Zhang aloud.

The assistant laughed. Li-Hong Zhang looked out the window into the Tientsin night.

There was more worrying to do before the sun came up.

* * *

Ulysses S. Grant stood in his chambers beside a table and chair with documents, smoking a cigar thoughtfully.

At the edge of the room sat his assistant, Holcombe.

A young woman entered the room. She wore a navy-blue dress with a white collar and a narrow silhouette, forsaking the full bustle that had been the fashion.

"Ah," said General Grant. "You must be Miss Topham."

"Thank you for seeing me, Mister President," she said. The President gave a bow, and she a curtsy.

"I am a linguist and a graduate of Brown University.

"I am cataloguing the Chinese dialects. I have come from Peking to see you."

President Grant seated her and took a chair across from her.

"As it happens, my uncle is the publisher of Stoddard and Sons. He has asked me to solicit the publication of your memoirs –

"As well as to offer my services as editor."

Before Grant could reply, she added, "The sum he is prepared to offer you is one hundred thousand dollars. For the domestic rights."

Both General Grant and Holcombe, in the periphery, stopped moving at the mention of this sum.

"As you may be aware, General Lee was offered less than half that amount for his memoirs. Stoddard and Sons are most eager to publish yours. My uncle has directed me to tell you this in no uncertain terms."

She removed a letter and placed it on the table.

"Half payable on advance. He specifies in the note that he can wire it into your Philadelphia bank within a day of receiving your assent."

"That is a most generous offer," said Ulysses S. Grant. "I don't know what I have to write that could be worth such a sum."

"Mister Pres—General Grant – you are … You are a world figure.

"The fees for the international rights would be equal to the domestic, or so my uncle has told me."

The 18th President spoke plainly, and favored strong verbs. He disdained most adjectives and all adverbs, as they hindered clarity.

"Robert Lee did not, in the end," recalled Grant, "write his memoirs."

She waited for him to complete the thought.

"I believe, in the end, he felt he could not do a full measure of justice to the men and to the cause so close to his heart."

"While it is true that a number of memoirs of the War have failed to ignite popular interest, and have been remaindered, Colonel Jackson' s biography has sold almost 300,000 copies. But, of course, he is a Rebel, so there is some special interest there.

The 18th President spoke plainly, and favored strong verbs. He disdained most adjectives and all adverbs, as they hindered clarity.

"And Patrick's autobiography has done very brisk business lately, with the anniversary of Kennesaw Mountain and all."

"We believe that with a bold structure, your book could -- "

"Structure?" asked Grant.

"Yes," said the industrious Miss Topham. "A framing concept. We do have an idea – a conceit, really – which the publisher seems to favor."

"I would like to hear it."

"Then here it is!" said Miss Topham. "My idea is to take your global visit and use it as a lens, or a scrim, to look back and tell your own story…"

Grant nodded.

"We would use your world tour as an organizing structure for your memoirs. It gives us the chance to build in the great themes.

"'Ulysses S. Grant in Paris' meets – and then we give an account of your time in the City of Lights, comparing you to Napoleon and Gettysburg to Waterloo, don't you see – it gives you the opportunity to explain your ideas on leadership, and contrast them with his.

"Then the chapter 'Ulysses S. Grant in Italy' allows you to comment on the Roman Empire.

"Then we build parallels between you and Julius Caesar -- "

"I see," commented General Grant.

"And then a section which will parallel Caesars' *Commentaries* … and of course compare Jefferson Davis to Caligula …"

"Caligula? Jefferson Davis?"

"Or not," said Miss Topham quickly. "It is only an example of the kind of latitude this framework gives us. The reader can follow all of your thoughts and theories, since they always know where they are. In the progression."

Miss Topham looked at Grant. He rolled the cigar in his hand.

"Then the chapter 'Ulysses S. Grant in India' delves into the untouchables," she continued, "a corollary which brings us of course to slaves, and to the American Civil War -- "

Grant began to protest.

"Your modesty is widely known, sir," she assured him, "and it is our belief that this grander structure would be a *tonic* or that is to say an *offset* to --

Grant held up his hand for her to stop as Mrs. Grant entered the study, reading mail.

"Hiram," said Mrs. Grant. "We have mail waiting for us. Buck is well and the grandchildren send their love."

"Just in time, dear. Miss Topham here was just comparing me to the Caesars. Another minute and I would be Charlemagne."

Mrs. Grant looked up.

"Oh! I beg your pardon."

Miss Topham bowed.

"And that nice Hindoo man," said Mrs. Grant to her husband, "we went tiger hunting with in Futtehpoor – Mister Bahadur. He is *dead*! Killed by a rolling elephant, apparently."

"And that nice Hindoo man," said Mrs. Grant to her husband, "Mister Bahadur, he is *dead!*"

"I found him somewhat fanatical," said Grant after a lengthy pause. He glanced at Holcombe.

"But an elephant – can you imagine. I will leave you alone. Good evening, Tom, you're awfully quiet there in the corner," she said to Holcombe, who smiled and offered a half-salute.

General Grant returned to the subject of writing his Civil War memoirs.

"There seem to be two schools of thought as regards to why history unfolds as it does," he said to Miss Topham.

"One school says that it is great forces which clash, with war and peace as byproducts. Drought and famine, progressions in science, medicine, economic shifts – animal migrations – these are the drivers of events.

"The second school of thought says that the great men dictate history. Henry XIII, Genghis Khan, Jesus – their will, their vision, their campaigns are the engines of history.

"My own feeling is that evil men in particular alter the course of these great rivers of change. The combustion points come and go if there is no John Brown, or John Calhoun, to ignite them."

"My own feeling is that evil men in particular alter the course of these great rivers of change ..."

Miss Topham nodded eagerly. “Yours is a combination of theories, then. You believe that great forces create the opportunity for war, but that it is exceptional men who light the fire. Men who are exceptionally good, or exceptionally bad.”

“Timing is the thing,” said Grant. “Wrong-headed men appearing at a critical time. They bring ruin.

“Eliminate those men, you may eliminate war. Stave it off for a decade or so, at least. Things have a way of changing. Eliminate certain individuals and you can prevent these mass-murder scenarios. Sacrifice a single life for many thousands.”

Eliminate certain individuals and you can prevent these mass-murder scenarios. Sacrifice a single life for many thousands.

They could hear faint music floating in from the square. Grant extinguished his cigar.

“While it is very clever, I do not feel I can embrace your global construct with sincerity, Miss Topham. Perhaps -- ”

“I was hoping to avoid saying this directly,” interrupted Miss Topham, “but the Publisher does truly prefer it. He will issue the advance only on the understanding that your memoirs are framed within this precept.” Nothing in her carriage or in the tone of her voice indicated deference to the greatest military leader of the 19th century.

A long silence ensued. A Union officer once said that Grant "habitually wears an expression as if he had determined to drive his head through a brick wall, and was about to do it." This is the expression he wore now, and his visitor understood that a decision had been made.

"After the Battle of Waterloo," said Grant, "Wellington made a simple request.

"He asked that no one ever attempt to write a history of that battle.

"They could never get it right, and in getting it wrong, they would dishonor his comrades.

"I suppose that's the way I feel."

Grant stood erect and bowed to his visitor.

"I am glad to have met you, Miss Topham. I wish you the best of luck."

"But – but I -- " She gathered herself for one last effort.

"I was led to believe by the Publisher that you … that your … your finances had -- "

"Become untenable? That is certainly true," said Grant. "This trip of ours will deplete the last of our savings."

"Then why not sign this agreement? Upon signing, a significant fortune will accrue then you can begin writing in the summer. I have ideas for — "

"I cannot sign your agreement," replied Grant.

"I do hope you enjoy the rest of your visit to Tientsin."

The mysterious aide, Holcombe, escorted the visitor to the door and the meeting was ended.

* * *

The teens were sleeping in a dormitory room, with bunks against the wall.

Pao Shan could not sleep. She sat at a small grated window, watching the moon.

L'uk Kun's face appeared at the window, his fingers spread on the open grate.

"Don't go tomorrow!" he whispered to Pau Shan. "There will be shooting!"

Deep emotions could be heard in his voice.

"Wait!" whispered Pao Shan

"You could have killed me," said L'uk Kun. "In the caves. The least I can do is warn you."

L'uk Kun's face appeared at the window. "Don't go tomorrow!" he whispered. "There will be shooting!"

"You mustn't! It's not safe --"

"You wouldn't understand."

"I – I understand," said Pao Shan.

"You have been told. Events will take their course. I can do no more."

Pao Shan hesitated, torn.

"Be careful ..."

But he was already gone.

PART V: THE CONCERT FOR ULYSSES S. GRANT

The quarter sat in the musicians' section along the curve of the stage

"We were terrible," moaned Soo Ching.

"We played well," corrected the Instructor.

"We got last place," said Ning Po, whose face had regained its natural color.

"We still have the closing ceremony," the Instructor reminded him.

"Can we go home and NOT do that --" aske Soo Ching.

"Aw, to hell with all of 'em!" exclaimed Joseph. "I *like* our music! It's jus' new to some ears -- "

"Perhaps some of the more … traditional musicians were able to, um, capture the judges' attention," admitted the Instructor thoughtfully. "But Pao Shan, your solo was the best you have ever done. And Soo Ching--"

The sharp bang of a gavel sounded.

The International Court of Tientsin opened session.

The setting was reminiscent of the Globe Theatre, with rows of staggered ampitheater seats surrounding a central stage.

On the stage, Ulysses S. Grant, acting as judge, sat on a throne-like chair. Holcombe stood beside two armed Union soldiers. Two others stood at the stage's edge.

Four delegations -- China, America, Japan and Ryukyu ("Loochoo") – sat around a huge wooden table at Center Stage.

Against the back wall and a great table at center stage, huge flags of the four nations hung down from the rafters. A gigantic clock kept time.

The Quartet sat among the orchestra, on stage. Beyond the seated dignitaries in the audience stood a gallery of swaying and moving spectators who strained to see and hear the proceedings.

The time on the wall clock was 1:47.

Li-Hong Zhang was in summary of his argument.

"So you see, General: China wishes only to continue its traditional role as friend and protector to the Ryukyu people.

"We have no ambitions towards the Kingdom's internal life.

"We wish only to trade with, and live in peace beside the island people.

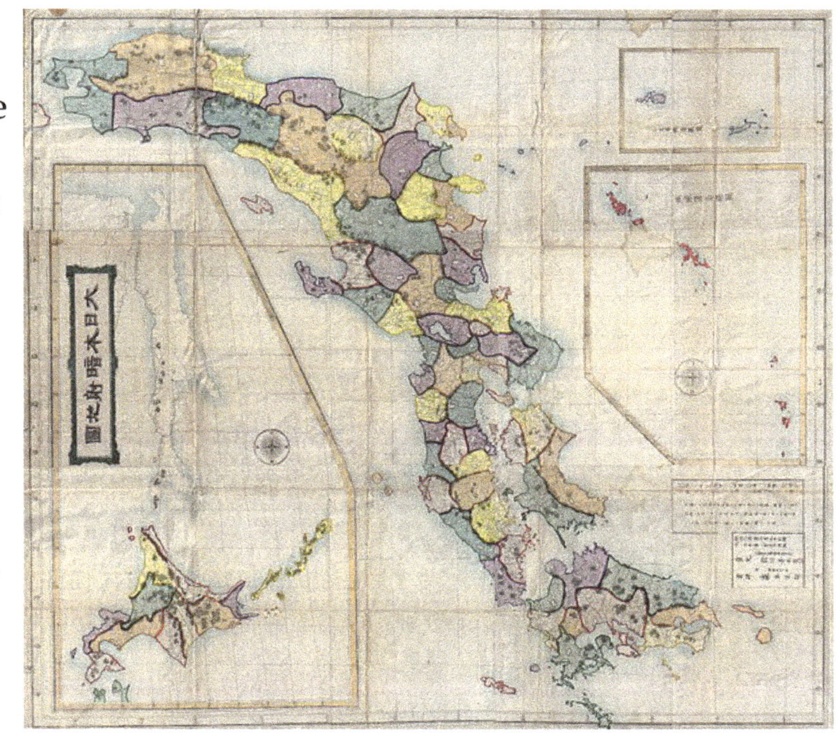

The Japanese representative, Sato, stood from his seat and walked to the center of the stage.

"This unfortunate situation is entirely my fault, Learned Ones," he declared.

"I humbly apologize."

Sato's unexpected statement created a stir.

"Our recent communique was mis-worded. Japan did not – of course! -- mean to levy a land tax on the people of Ryukyu."

He bowed to the Ryukyu delegation.

Yobu, the Ryukyudelegation leader, looked on suspiciously.

"It was our intention," continued Sato smoothly, "to suggest these sums as a commercial fee for our ships' rights-of-passage in the Straits."

Yobu leapt to his feet.

"And what a sum! Thirty thousand *ryo*! annually!"

"That is not the case," denied Sato. "There is confusion due to the complexity of the gold-convertible paper money we now term *daijokansatsu*."

"So you say!" Yobu's face was red with anger. "Japan seeks a tariff. China seeks control of all the surrounding waters. Together, it would spell the end for our tiny nation!"

"The amount is far less than the Counselor fears," said Sato, the Japanese, wisely ignoring the larger charge.

"The Straits must remain forever free! Ryukyuan monarchs have defended the islands against invaders since the Mongols seven centuries ago," warned Yobu. "We will do it again. If necessary!"

"There was no intent to show disrespect," said the Japanese minister.

Now Yobu, of Ryukyu, addressed General Grant.

"Most recently, the Japanese Emperor hasrecommended that our children be taught in Japanese. Will the Ryukyu Kingdoms soon become the Ryukyu Province … a fiefdom of Japan?"

"It is a gesture to encourage cultural amity among our peoples," explained Sato, the Japanese. "Only a suggestion."

"And now you have 'suggested' a law banning our people from owning swords!" cried Yobu. "Shall we fight with frying pans? Sewing needles?

"It is a naked ploy by our powerful enemies to disarm us, so we will be defenseless against them."

"Defend against what?" Sato spread his arms, to imply he had nothing to hide. "Do we have an army assembled on your borders that I am unaware of?"

The Ryukyu ambassador made no reply to this.

General Grant spoke. "The Imperial warships *Kotetsu* and *Hashimidate* moved into Okinawa waters earlier this week, I understand."

At this news, a stir moved among the audience. Such a sophisticated statement reflected an understanding beyond that of a casual observer.

The time on the giant clock now measured 1:51.

"Equipped with twelve-inch Canet guns," added General Grant. "While six of your frigates wait in the sea caves just north of Nawa Harbor."

Murmurs and protests were heard in the gallery.

Sato's voice had a new, cautious tone to it. "How is it that the American General is so well informed on … minor movements in the Sea of Japan?"

"Surely, a close knowledge of the maritime is a universal good," replied Grant. "I am in the acquaintance of a retired navigator or two."

"Our ships only move to Okinawa to rendezvous with the French," explained Sato.

"All know that the French ships do the Japanese bidding," said Grant, implacably.

"The law regarding weapons," said Grant. "Who wrote this new law, counselor? Was it Eisaku? Was it a council of some kind?"

"I myself composed it," answered Sato.

"I see," said Grant.

"It is thus for our own citizens," shrugged Sato. "We treat our friends just as we treat our own citizens. Is this wrong?

"We believe it is an honor for the citizens of the Kingdom to also become citizens of the Empire of the Rising Sun," said Sato.

"Especially in coming times, when our flag will fly higher and ever higher over the lands of the East."

"Exactly what does that mean?" asked Grant.

"Only that each culture has its place in the scheme of things," answered the Japanese consul. "Japan's place is to help. To organize. To lend structure. To … to lead. We seek merely to fulfill our destiny. *Tenno Heika Bansai!*"

He saluted the flag of the Rising Sun, perched high on the wall.

"I see," murmured the American General.

"I don't think you do see," replied Sato." In your own nation's case, General Grant … did the U. S. government ask permission from the Cher-o-kee before they took over the Kansas lands?"

Hearing this, Minister Yobu shot to his feet.

"We know when we are being invaded!" The crowd murmured, both at the direct challenge to Grant and the explosion from Yobu.

"Was there not an assumption that the Americans," Sato continued, "could put the land to better use than the Cher-o-kee? That it was your right to do so?

"Surely you can see that this is no different. We – the Japanese – feel that we can help put the resources to better use. It is our destiny to do so."

"More so than the Chinese?" asked Li Hong Zhang. He had hoped to play neutral in this game, but China and her interests could hardly be forgotten.

"*Gaw seong nga hang yaw tiu low?*" demanded Yobu on behalf of the Ryukyu Kingdom.

Zhang chose his words carefully. "When a race … when a race has *consolidated*, as is the case with Japan, then all things are possible. It is not …" he shrugged, as though he could not capture the thought correctly, "… the Chinese are distracted. By their many tribes. And tribal interests. And by the opium. As you see."

Ulysses S. Grant had heard enough.

He rose from his throne-like chair to interrupt the argument before it escalated.

He stood to address the court, signaling an end to the oral presentations. He would now render his decision.

Li Hong Zhang glanced up. The time on the giant wall clock was now 1:54

"Gentlemen, I thank you," said Grant.

"Your eloquence and your logic do honor to your people.

"Your arguments are all sound.

"I do not know that we can resolve all of the issues you raise.

"When the Viceroy first suggested that I adjudicate this matter, I declined. The judgment had no power of enforcement.

"Now, I understand that all three parties have signed an agreement to abide by what we conclude here today. My decision is binding. My ruling stands as law for no less than three years. Is that correct?"

He turned to face each delegation. All parties nodded.

"Is that still agreeable?"

All parties agreed.

"I have felt the passions that charge this room before," said the hero of Vicksburg somberly.

"The looks on the faces in this chamber, today – I have seen looks like that on men before.

"War walks in this room like a living thing. It stands among us as surely as the air we breathe.

"The type of hell you wish to unleash is *one you will each live to regret*.

"I would sooner shoot any ten of you gentle folk right here, in the head, rather than let you open such a Pandora's Box upon the countryside."

The crowd was surprised by this dark talk. An uneasy thrum rippled through the delegations and the audience, particularly those standing at the rear and on the balconies. Several more Union soldiers appeared along the stage's edge.

"But such warnings are useless," continued Grant. "Pride will win the day. Events will take their course."Here is my decision. None will be fully pleased. None will be pleased, yet all will gain. In equal measure, I hope.

"The annual payment from Ryukyu to China is no longer a tribute but a fee. A fee paid in exchange for safe transit.

"The amount is to be reduced to twenty thousand *daijokansatsu* annually.

"Similarly, the Kingdom's payment to Japan will not be a tax at all but a commercial agreement. A rendering for services. Twenty thousand *ryo*.

"Japan will forfeit the islands of Miyako and Yaeyama."

Li Hong Zhang's eyebrows rose at this.

The Ryukyu delegation began to stand and cheer at this, but Grant held out his arm for silence.

"Ryukyu will permit Japanese citizens to visit freely," he continued, "with or without Shogunate permission."

Minster Sato nodded smugly.

"As to the fishing rights," declared Grant, "those are denied Japan. A separate fee for specific rights can be negotiated directly between prefectures."

The hands on the wall clock clicked to 1:58.

"As to access to the sea channels -- "

"General!" cried Joseph. "Above you!"

"There he is!" echoed Soo Ching.

Following the boys' gestures, the crowd saw a running figure descending the tiers of spectators as he made his way towards the dignitaries.

It was L'uk Kun.

"Si gap ma hang tin!" called Pao Shan desperately.

Nearing the stage even as guards from three directions moved to seize him, Lu'k Kun removed a pistol from his cumberbund.

Then turned sharply, away from the American delegation, and headed straight for the Chinese dignitaries --

He drew and aimed his weapon.

"They're after the Viceroy!" called General Grant to his troops, directing them to leave him and protect his host.

"Joseph! No!" cried Ning Po.

Five important things happened at once:

The giant clock struck two o'clock.

Joseph leapt up from his chair and ran towards Li Hong Zhang. He threw himself in front of the Viceroy.

General Grant stood and bellowed, "Viceroy!"

Viceroy Li Hong Zhang removed a hand-gun from his vest to defend himself.

"Holcombe!" cried Grant. "My pistol!"

A gun exploded with a startling *Boom!*

"*Gong ji,* Mister President!" shouted Holcombe--

Soldiers converged on both General Grant and the Viceroy.

The delegations erupted in shouting and a turmoil of motion. Ning Po rushed to the stage.

A second pistol cracked, then a third.

Lu'k Kun leapt from the balcony onto the great conference table and shot again at the Viceroy.

The crowd converged in a melee.

Many shots rang out. The greatchamber was engulfed in chaos and panic for an extended moment.

Just as quickly as it formed, the panic receded.

The crowd settled. The crowded stage gradually calmed, and cleared enough that the entire hall could now see that it was not Viceroy Li Hong Zhang who had been shot but the Japanese legate, Sato. He lay in his compatriots' arms, his chest red and heaving.

"Why?" wailed a Japanese delegate. Why would a Chinese rebel target a Japanese -- ?"

Yet Sato lived.

Ulysses S. Grant was safe.

Li Hong Zhang was angry, but safe.

Joseph, who had leapt in front of the Chinese Viceroy, was wounded in the leg.

L'uk Kun, who had shot at the Chinese Viceroy, was wounded but alive enough to shout curses at Li Hong Zhang. Pao Shan tended to him while guards took him away.

Minister Sato was able to sit up, and gave a sign to his delegation, which cheered.

Li Hong Zhang asked the Instructor to commence playing, in the hope that the music would help soothe the hall.

She began to play, hesitantly at first.

A Scotsman joined in, his bagpipe creating a startling accompaniment to her melody.

One by one, other musicians picked up the tune.

The music rose. The wounds were bandaged. Sato was carried from the stage.

Slowly, the mood changed.

Soo Ching stood and walked to the front of the stage, so all could see him, and hear his playing.

Ning Po stood beside him, leading the musicians and urging them to join in.

Joseph, his leg bandaged, added his harmonica to the chorus.

The great hall was filled with musicians of many nations playing the Chinese folk tune, a surprisingly durable melody.

New blends of rhythms and harmonies ensued.

The Ryuku minister, Yobu, took the arms of Japanese delegate and began to dance.

Li Hong Zhang followed suit.

The raucous American delegation demanded it, and General Grant performed a jig. He waved his cigar. He seemed to smile. He dropped the cigar and found his wife to dance with him, there beneath the flags.

The curtains behind the stage were drawn away to reveal two armchairs on a pedestal, with a small table and a vase of flowers between.

A photographer and a gigantic camera with lights were made ready.

The two leaders climbed the pedestal to pose. The lights flared and popped.

"Again!" said Ning Po, and a new and more ragged, more robust verse of the music started up. There was laughing among the musicians from the German delegation, and the Spaniards with their colorful drums could not help march around the chamber in time to the music.

"We win!" cried Soo Ching.

"That was beautiful," said the Instructor, over the din, to her trio (for Pao Shan would not leave L'uk's side). "Your music has won their hearts."

"You're a damn fool, Hiram," said Mrs. Grant, most pleased.

"Perhaps another time," said Holcombe, so no one could hear. He adjusted the pistol in his belt, in the back, and covered it with his tuxedo jacket.

"We hold fast to our purpose," said Ulysses S. Grant.

At the photographer's command, the two leaders looked into the camera.

"We hold fast."

The photographer's flash went off.

Archival photograph of Ulysses S. Grant and Viceroy Li-Hong Zhang

AFTERWORD

(1879) Tientsin, China
Two remarkable leaders meet during an era of modernization and drastic realignments

In the year 1877, after leaving the White House, Ulysses S. Grant embarked on a two-year trip around the world. He and his small entourage were received with great ceremony in capitals across Europe and Asia.

In March of 1878, they arrived in Peking, where General Grant met the Chinese Viceroy and politician Li Hong Zhang. Zhang asked Grant to serve as arbiter over a dispute between China and Japan as to the conservatorship of the Ryukyu ("Loochoo") Island Kingdom.

In this fictional account, a student musical group has been asked to play for Grant and the international dignitaries of Tientsin. When an American youth (Joseph) joins the concert group, jealousies and secrets among the teenaged players are revealed. The youths' powerful emotions are expressed through seven brief musical pieces. The music takes on new aspects and changing dynamics as the two cultures – American and Chinese, monarchical and democratic – come together.

Matters more serious than teenage rivalries take over when an assassination plot comes to light. Opium, gun smuggling, and the colonial forces of class and rebellion all play a part in the surprising climax of the five short acts of "Ulysses S. Grant in China."

As the adventure opens, the three Chinese music students, their new American friend, and the rebel boy they have captured are climbing the hills above the city. They have just escaped a shocking scene in which their father was revealed to be both a traitor and an abusive husband. They are being chased by both the Imperial police and the rebels who would soon fire the Boxer Rebellion.

The English spelling of 'Li Hong Zhang' could take many forms. The Chinese language in this story is unvetted.

* * *

Ulysses S. Grant was one of the most extraordinary military leaders in American history … this much has been pretty much the consensus.

As President, not so extraordinary. In fact, he has often been rated as among the least-effective politicians. Historians viewed his attempts to implement Reconstruction as failures, and the clouds of scandal over his tenure have never really lifted.

In recent years, this view has changed. Grant's reputation is in the middle of an upgrade. Scholars like Josiah Bunting and Frank Scaturro have argued in recent books and articles that we may have been looking at Grant through a flawed lens. "Only more recently have historians begun to appreciate Grant's commitment to African Americans," states the Miller Center for Presidential History. Ron Chernow's well-received 2017 biography of Grant portrays him, as one reviewer writes, to be "self-made, hard-working, modest for himself and ambitious for his nation, future-looking, tolerant, and with a heart for the poor."

Japanese depiction of American warshipWikimedia Commons

* * *

The mysterious events and philosophy at the heart of this story revolve around the idea that Grant was eliminating key war-mongers in the kingdoms he visited. Grant strikes me as a figure who has seen more than his share of melancholy. He has seen more of war's devastation than anyone. He wishes to stop it in other lands before it starts.

This has absolutely zero basis in fact.

* * *

I came across a photograph of Ulysses S. Grant and Li Hong Zhang sitting in twin thrones, in China, in 1877 and I could not get the clash of cultures out of my mind. This story is the result. My hope was to balance the big themes of the two nations' histories against the pragmatic (and sad -- always sad) personalities of Grant and Li Hong Zhang.

I have always imagined it as a play, with music. My early speechy drafts had a gruff ex-president drinking too much, remembering Robert E. Lee and the Battle of Shiloh, and generally contemplating large matters. Terrible. This draft, I hope, is livelier. I have several more to go.

Two of the young characters here might connect this story to a new story I have in mind about the Boxer Rebellion, twenty years after Grant's visit.

* * *

You and I need to know more about China.

Li Hong Zhang is a powerful figure in modern China's history, yet when I first saw that photo, I had never heard of him. One of the reasons he is so pivotal is because he sought to manage China's uneasy relationship with the West. He also succeeded in balancing Asian power politics, between Japan's expansionist young Emperor Meiji and an assertive Russia, looking for ever-wider influence. Sound familiar?

Japan's aggressive Pacific strategy, which you see in the full-text version of "Ulysses S. Grant in China," is a seen as a precursor to the total-Pacific domination plan of World War II. The relationship between China and Japan is ancient, complex, and passionate, and one that bears significance in our own times.

Related reading can be found in the free journal article "Partnership for Disorder" (www.empirestudies.com). This feature looks at Xiaoyuan Liu's fascinating profile of the brief partnership between China and the U.S. as they teamed up against Japan in the period 1941-45. It was a partnership full of promise, vast ambition, and misunderstanding. Once more, this is a good thing to know as our two governments attempt to coordinate strategies.

CHARACTERS
Pao-Shan = working class girl (servant's daughter, age 15)
Ning Po = rich girl (age 16)
Soo Ch'ing = little brother of Ning Po (age 14)

Madame Xi Ping = Ning Po's mother, beautiful, frail, haunted
Pi Chin = Madame Xi Ping's attendant and Pao Shan's mother
The Instructor = gifted in music but perhaps naïve in the ways of the world
Joseph Seward = American boy (age 17)
Luk K'un = Rebel boy (age 15)

Viceroy Li Hong Zhang = himself
General Ulysses S. Grant = himself
Holcombe = Grant's aide

Miss Topham = Publisher's representative
Sato = Japanese representative in the Loochoo negotiations
Yobu = Ryukyu representative in the Loochoo negotiations

AUTHOR BIO

Tom Durwood is a teacher, writer and editor with an interest in history. Tom most recently taught English Composition and Empire and Literature at Valley Forge Military College, where he won the *Teacher of the Year* Award five times. Tom has taught Public Speaking and Basic Communications as guest lecturer for the Naval Special Warfare Development Group at the Dam's Neck Annex of the Naval War College.

Tom's ebook *Empire and Literature* matches global works of film and fiction to specific quadrants of empire, finding surprising parallels. Literature, film, art and architecture are viewed against the rise and fall of empire. In a foreword to *Empire and Literature*, postcolonial scholar Dipesh Chakrabarty of the University of Chicago calls it "imaginative and innovative." Prof. Chakrabarty writes that "Durwood has given us a thought-provoking introduction to the humanities." His subsequent book "Kid Lit: An Introduction to Literary Criticism" has been well-reviewed. "My favorite nonfiction book of the year," writes The Literary Apothecary (Goodreads).

Early reader response to Tom's historical fiction adventures has been promising. "A true pleasure … the richness of the layers of Tom's novel is compelling," writes Fatima Sharrafedine in her foreword to "The Illustrated Boatman's Daughter." The Midwest Book Review calls that same title "uniformly gripping and educational … pairing action and adventure with social issues." Adds Prairie Review, "A deeply intriguing, ambitious historical fiction series."

Tom's newspaper column "Shelter" appeared in the *North County Times* for seven years. Tom earned a Masters in English Literature in San Diego, where he also served as Executive Director of San Diego Habitat for Humanity.

Tom briefly ran his own children's book imprint, Calico Books (Contemporary Books, Chicago). His name can occasionally be found in footnotes of obscure scholarly works, in conjunction with his undergraduate arts journal.

ILLUSTRATORS

Zelda Devon
Currently based in Los Angeles, Zelda Devon creates visuals for the entertainment industry. She has 15 years of experience in advertising, and has published with Random House, Scholastic and Disney. Zelda places her focus on rich storytelling through movement and vibrant color, evoking a sense of magic and whimsy to visually captivate the viewer.

Dominik Mayer is a German concept artist and illustrator,currently working in Nuremberg. He has worked on video and board games such *Magic the Gathering* and *Legends of Honor*. His artwork brings the story "Origins of Civilization" to life in this collection.

'Dreamcatcher' by Zelda Davon

Timothy Mathon, whose illustrations are featured in the title story, is a French artist who has worked with Net Ease Games, Ubisoft Annecy, Quantic Dream. He teaches at Bellecour Ecole in Lyon.

Boell Oyino has worked in a number of fields – video games, animation, (Amazon Game Studios and Hibernian Workshop), comics and manga. Among the many titles he has contributed to is *Forest of Liars*.

Sigurd Fernstrom lives in Stockholm, Sweden. Sigurd has worked as Senior Concept Artist at DICE and Concept Artist at Important Looking Pirates, among other credits.

Well-bee is the pen name for a rising young comic book artist and illustrator from Serbia.

The Illustrated Boatman's Daughter

A girl of the Nile fights corruption to help build the Suez Canal

Timing is everything. In the summer of 1874, sixteen-year-old Salima wishes desperately to escape her mundane life on the Nile. As the world flocks to Egypt for the construction of the Suez Canal, the great waterway which will join East and West, Salima emerges into a world swirling with powerful imperial forces. Against all odds, Salima and her friends Emilie and Mikal (and Salima's beloved collie, Fadil) stand against the empires who seek to colonize Egypt.

By a twist of fate, Salima and her new friend Emile are recruited to help the Dutch, and are drawn into a shadowy world surrounding the Suez Canal construction. As she circulates through Cairo and the lands beyond, Salima discovers that her people have been enslaved to dig the canal, working without food, pay or respite. She demands fair treatment, lobbying for decent wages and safe working conditions—an unexpected heroine to the people of Egypt.

A second, more nefarious plot comes to light when it's revealed that the project's European financiers have swindled the Egyptians, and unless the terms can be changed, France and Britain will own Egypt's jewel and likely her people as well.

Salima and Emilie travel south, to the Valley of Kings, to outsmart the assassins who stalk them. They encounter Khalid, the young rebel leader of the desert tribes. Growing love interests among the band of teen companions threatens to tear them apart, until a mysterious stranger helps them bring the past alive in order to save Egypt's future.

"A true pleasure ... the richness of the layers of Tom's novel is compelling. The forty pieces of art complete the experience. The events of this adventure story progress fast. Confrontations take drastic turns. Salima is a heroine in the true sense. She is captivating."

From the Foreword by Fatima Sharrafedine

Kid Lit: An Introduction to Literary Criticism

An award-winning teacher lays out the basic rules of literary criticism in this accessible guide.

We are surrounded by narratives, in fiction and in our everyday lives. In this colorful collection of ideas, the author argues that understanding the components of our favorite children's stories can lead to a lifetime of critical thinking.

Beginning with the elements of the universal coming-of-age narrative, "Kid Lit" shows young readers and general readers alike how to recognize story structure, class, gender, symbolism, trauma and Orientalism in children's narratives.

Of value to all teachers, students, librarians, readers, literature lovers, and moviegoers.

Tom Durwood expertly breaks down and explains literary theory in an easy-to-understand way. This book makes sense of reading critically and guides students to producing their own explanations of literature.

-- *Christine E. Carlson, English Instructor, Cabrini University*

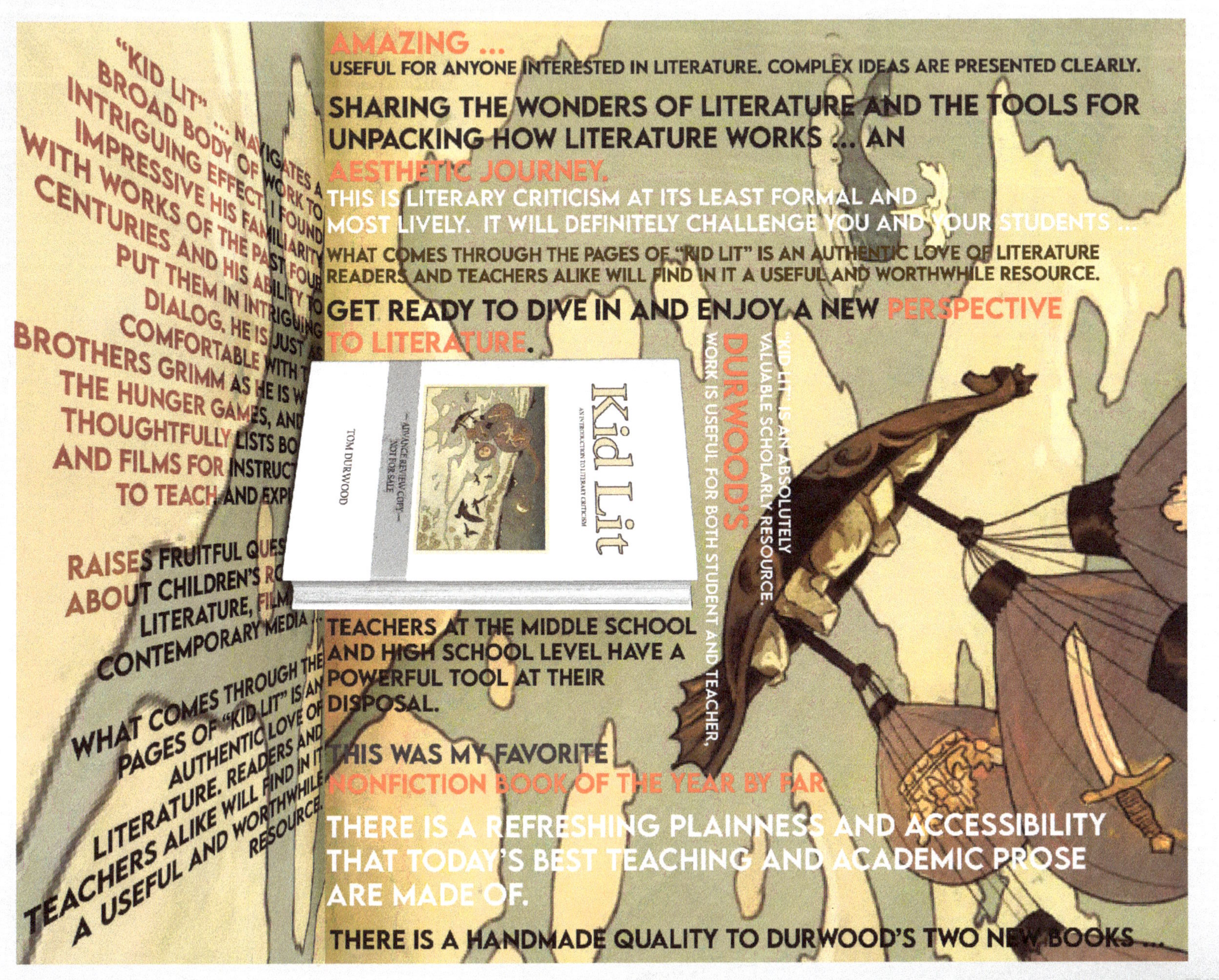
AMAZING ...
USEFUL FOR ANYONE INTERESTED IN LITERATURE. COMPLEX IDEAS ARE PRESENTED CLEARLY.
SHARING THE WONDERS OF LITERATURE AND THE TOOLS FOR UNPACKING HOW LITERATURE WORKS ... AN AESTHETIC JOURNEY.
THIS IS LITERARY CRITICISM AT ITS LEAST FORMAL AND MOST LIVELY. IT WILL DEFINITELY CHALLENGE YOU AND YOUR STUDENTS ...
WHAT COMES THROUGH THE PAGES OF "KID LIT" IS AN AUTHENTIC LOVE OF LITERATURE READERS AND TEACHERS ALIKE WILL FIND IN IT A USEFUL AND WORTHWHILE RESOURCE.
GET READY TO DIVE IN AND ENJOY A NEW PERSPECTIVE TO LITERATURE.
"KID LIT" IS AN ABSOLUTELY VALUABLE SCHOLARLY RESOURCE.
DURWOOD'S WORK IS USEFUL FOR BOTH STUDENT AND TEACHER,
Kid Lit
AN INTRODUCTION TO LITERARY CRITICISM
— ADVANCE REVIEW COPY — NOT FOR SALE
TOM DURWOOD
TEACHERS AT THE MIDDLE SCHOOL AND HIGH SCHOOL LEVEL HAVE A POWERFUL TOOL AT THEIR DISPOSAL.
THIS WAS MY FAVORITE NONFICTION BOOK OF THE YEAR BY FAR
THERE IS A REFRESHING PLAINNESS AND ACCESSIBILITY THAT TODAY'S BEST TEACHING AND ACADEMIC PROSE ARE MADE OF.
THERE IS A HANDMADE QUALITY TO DURWOOD'S TWO NEW BOOKS ...

Kid Lit

AN INTRODUCTION TO LITERARY CRITICISM

TOM DURWOOD

The Illustrated Boatman's Daughter

BY TOM DURWOOD

ILLUSTRATED BY

Serena Malyon
Niklas Frostgard
Faustine Dumontier
Oliver Ryan
Devin Korwin
Kevin Fleeman
Ardalan Izanian
Zelda Devon

www.ingramcontent.com/pod-product-compliance
Lightning Source LLC
Chambersburg PA
CBHW042104160726
48295CB00017B/977

* 9 7 8 1 9 5 2 5 2 0 1 0 5 *